Rescued

by

Priscilla West

Table of Contents

Chapter One *FALLOUT*

Chapter Two *A NEW HOME*

Chapter Three *HEALTHY*

Chapter Four *AWKWARD*

Chapter Five *A NEW MORNING*

Chapter Six MEMORIES

Chapter Seven *MOVING ON*

Chapter Eight *HELP*

Chapter Nine *FUN AND GAMES*

Chapter Ten *PERFECT*

Chapter Eleven *SECRETS*

Chapter Twelve *TALK*

Chapter Thirteen *A DIFFERENT KIND OF READING*

Chapter Fourteen *STOLEN MOMENTS*

Chapter Fifteen *STRONG*

Chapter Sixteen *CLINT*

Chapter Seventeen *PROGRESS*

Chapter Eighteen AN INVITATION

Chapter Nineteen *NEW BEGINNINGS*

Chapter Twenty *WAKE*

Chapter Twenty-one *CHANGES*

Chapter Twenty-two *HELP*

Chapter Twenty-three *FRONT DESK*

Chapter Twenty-four *DISTRACTION*

Chapter Twenty-five *ANSWERS*

Chapter Twenty-six *TOSS AND TURN*

Chapter Twenty-seven *WHAT'S MINE TO KNOW*

Chapter Twenty-eight *STORM*

Chapter Twenty-nine *CLOSURE*

Epilogue

Chapter One
FALLOUT

"Tell me about Hunter."

I sat up on the plush tan couch in Dr. Schwartz's office and tried to catch my breath. The spasming muscles in my chest fought back bitterly.

Hunter. The mention of his name was enough to drive me to the edge of a panic attack.

"Lorrie? Would you like something?"

I shook my head and lay back down. The room was painted in creamy off-white and lit by lamps that glowed in soothing tones. Every decorative choice had been made with the goal of calming patients down. Patients like me.

The only exception to this rule was the ticking made by the clock on Dr. Schwartz's stained ash desk, in front of which she was seated. By my guess she was about a yard from where my feet were on the couch.

That ticking sound I could do without. Its steadiness made me nervous.

My thoughts raced anxiously as I thought about how to answer her. I'd just told her about everything that had happened in the days before I left Studsen. My face felt warm. The intensity of reliving all of that after days of lying numb in bed and trying not to feel anything was exhausting.

Now she was asking about Hunter. How should I answer that? He made me feel the best I'd ever felt. And the worst. It didn't really matter what I thought about him at this point. I was probably never going to see him again.

"Lorrie?" Dr. Schwartz asked, after a little while. "Can you tell me more about Hunter? You can start anywhere."

I took a deep breath again, the tension in my chest fighting back. Moisture started welling up in my eyes to my frustration. It would be messy if I cried. That morning I'd gotten a little enthusiastic with my makeup in anticipation of actually leaving the house for the first time since I'd returned to Indiana. It probably hadn't been the best idea to make myself up right before going to my therapist.

"Can I have a tissue?" I said, my voice quivering.

She handed me a tissue and I dabbed at my eyes, trying to get a hold of myself. My ribs seized against every attempt to fill my lungs. I'd been numb all week, but it was hard to hold back the emotions now.

Reality was settling in. I had left him beaten and broken. Hunter was out of my life and no one was going to save me from this nightmare.

"He keeps his apartment very clean," I said finally. "And he smells good."

The clock ticked and my heart beat erratically. Dr. Schwartz sat listening. After a few more deep breaths and who knows how many ticks of the clock on her desk, I continued. "He took me to his apartment after he saved me when I fell in a lake," I said in a small voice. "That's how we met. His place was so neat and tidy. It wasn't what I expected when I first saw him."

I almost smiled lying on the couch and thinking about that first day. I'd scurried across campus with his trash bag because I couldn't find a place to throw it out. My hands had been absolutely freezing by the time I got back to my dorm and threw it away. When I got back to my dorm room, I realized the sweatshirt I stole from him smelled wonderful. I lounged around in it for the rest of the day and hadn't even taken it off to sleep that night. That was so long ago.

Dr. Schwartz nodded encouragement. "What did you expect when you went to Hunter's apartment?" she asked. "Picture him for me on that day. What does he look like?"

"He looks like a bad boy . . ." I started. Tears again threatened to burst through, and I took a minute to calm myself. "But he's . . ." I tried to get more out, but every time I started to form a word I came close to crying. My entire body felt like a dam ready to burst.

"I knew things would get messed up between us," I croaked finally. "That's why I tried to hold back."

My therapist looked at me over her horn-rimmed glasses and her face screwed up at my last statement. She wrote something on her pad and nodded to herself.

I watched her for a moment, hoping this would be one of the rare times she said something, but she sat back in her chair and continued to gaze at me patiently. She had straight, graying hair that stopped just above her shoulders and was wearing her usual business suit, this time in herringbone.

After a while I realized she wasn't going to tell me what she had nodded about. I didn't feel like volunteering any more about Hunter, and so we sat there in silence for a couple minutes, each second marked out by the interminable clock on her desk.

The crushing numbness of the last few days began to return, along with my confusion. Every time I thought about what happened with Hunter, I hit a wall. We probably should have never gotten involved. Either I should have been stronger and stayed away, or I should have admitted my feelings for him sooner. What had happened had been a disaster.

It was exhausting to talk about it. The only other person I had told about what had happened was Daniela.

"Let's back up," my therapist said, breaking the silence. "Tell me about your semester. How was it for you being back at school?"

I took a deep breath, a little more freely this time. "I don't know," I said. "Hard, I guess. Classes were going okay but not great before the letter. I was drawing a lot. All I wanted was to be a normal student for one semester without any breakdowns."

Another silence followed, punctuated only by the clock. When I first started seeing Dr. Schwartz, silences like these made me feel awkward, but by this point I accepted them. She was just being patient and making sure I had nothing else to say. This wasn't a conversation. It was therapy.

"You've talked about getting back to normal before," she said. "Do you think you would have had a normal semester if you hadn't met Hunter?"

I flinched inwardly at his name. "Maybe. I guess I'll never know."

She waited.

"I would have gotten the letter from Marco either way," I said quietly, half to myself. "I don't know. That would have been bad with or without Hunter. Marco's going to haunt me forever, I think."

There was another pause. The clock ticked as I got more and more frustrated with everything that had happened. A terrible crushing sensation pressed against my chest and it was getting difficult to breathe.

"Seriously, what the hell?" I cried. "Who has to deal with someone ruining their life like this? It's ridiculous, isn't it? Why would he write me a letter?"

I clenched my jaw bitterly. Every time I thought about Marco it got me worked up.

"What did Hunter do after you got the letter from your stepfather?" Dr. Schwartz asked.

I pressed my knees together and bit my lip. "Nothing. He never found out."

"Oh. Did you hide it from him?"

I shook my head. "We didn't really talk for a few days. I have no idea why he didn't contact me."

I bit my tongue before saying any more. The way things had happened in my last few days at Arrowhart made me upset and confused. Dr. Schwartz didn't say anything, so I changed the subject back to Marco. "I just don't understand why he's out to ruin my life," I said. "How can you be normal when someone killed your mom, basically killed your dad, and then holds it over you like some kind of psychopath? And I'll never know why he did it."

Another minute was punctuated by the steady clock. My pulse raced faster and faster.

"How am I supposed to feel?" I cried, before sighing with frustration. Then I pushed my lips together and stayed quiet until she spoke.

"Do you think you would feel better about what happened to your parents if you knew why Marco killed your mother?"

"Yes," I said instantly.

"Have you asked him?"

My stomach sank. Ask him? Like he was just going to tell me after showing no remorse even during sentencing?

The clock ticked. Dr. Schwartz was waiting for my answer.

"They asked him during the trial," I tried. "Interrogated. Even during sentencing."

More time passed. "So then I understand you have not asked him personally. It might be worth considering. I know it would be deeply painful, but if you get answers it could be worthwhile. He may respond differently to your personal request than he did in a legal setting."

I took a few deep breaths. The prospect of writing Marco a letter back, even if it was just that question, was daunting. I really just wanted him and everything he did to me to go away.

"I'd like to return to Hunter," she said after a few more ticks of the interminable clock had passed. "Are you angry because he wasn't there to support you when you got the letter from Marco?"

Her voice was irritatingly steady, calm, and really getting on my nerves. "I thought this was about Marco," I said through my teeth.

My therapist didn't answer. I sat up to look at her and found she was staring at me neutrally.

Frustrated, I let myself fall back down and breathed out. "I don't want to talk about Hunter right now," I said, my voice beginning to shake. I tried changing the subject. "The most positive thing about the semester has been my drawing. That was basically the only thing I was good at."

I poked my head up and looked at her. Nothing. I might as well have been talking to an empty room. The emotion that had been bound up in my body threatened to overflow. I let myself back down onto the couch harder than I'd meant to.

"Maybe I shouldn't have gone back to Arrowhart," I said. "What happened after I got the letter was scary."

I chanced a glance at her and found the same attentive gaze.

"It was like I couldn't quite wake up from a bad nightmare," I said. "For a while, I kept hearing or seeing Marco and then realizing it was just in my head."

There wasn't much else to say. Once I'd read the letter from Marco I was basically useless for a few days. I hadn't even been able to read the questions on my psychology test. I had to recover.

Dr. Schwartz frowned. "I was worried when you left about the possibility of post-traumatic stress symptoms like those you've described. Of course, I didn't anticipate a trigger as direct as the one you received. It sounds like it took quite a toll on you."

I nodded.

"Thank you for sharing that. However, you avoided my question. Are you angry with Hunter?"

"Why do you keep trying to make this about him?" I snapped, blinking away fresh tears. "I told you I don't want to talk about that."

She paused for a moment before answering my question. "Because you're willing to talk about anything to avoid talking about Hunter, Lorrie. You're avoiding something important."

I bit my lip, waiting for her to say more, but nothing came. I took a few ragged breaths, trying to steady myself. Tears welled up big in my eyes and began to roll down my cheeks until a massive sob built up in my chest and crashed through my body.

Tears that had been building up since the moment I left Studsen poured out faster than I could wipe them.

The whole situation was just too much. Every time I tried to process it, I was overwhelmed.

When I looked toward Dr. Schwartz, I saw she had extended the tissue box to me. I tried to use a tissue to clean myself up, but it was no use. So much for looking presentable.

As soon as I pulled the tissue box away, tears began to stream from my eyes anew. "I don't know if I'm angry at Hunter or just confused," I mumbled unsteadily. "The whole thing doesn't make any sense."

For the first time since the appointment started, I wondered how long I had left before we were done for the day.

"I mean, what was I supposed to do? After he left me crying in front of the health center, I waited at his apartment to talk to him for hours. I couldn't have waited any longer."

The clock ticked. Again and again.

"Do you feel guilty, Lorrie?"

Anxious chills squirmed through my body. I had been arguing with myself for a week, trying to find a way this wasn't my fault. Even if I didn't deserve all the blame, maybe I did feel guilty.

"I don't know," I said, my voice barely my own. "Maybe."

After a short silence, I continued. "I shouldn't have left him when he was hurt. That's what I feel bad about. I should have stuck around and talked to him. Made sure he was okay."

My stomach was queasy. Saying the words I'd been feeling in the back of my mind was both liberating and upsetting. Fresh tears came, and this time I didn't even try to stop them. "But I didn't know what to do," I said again.

"It's alright to be confused," my therapist said. "But you shouldn't be avoiding what happened either. Is that all you feel guilty about? The way you left, I mean."

I licked my lips, thinking about how I wanted to phrase my answer to that question. "Well, and getting involved in the first place," I tried. I thought of what Gary had said at the fight. Had our relationship always been unhealthy?

"Like I said before, I should have either backed off totally or started a relationship sooner. The way I handled it was kind of the worst of both worlds."

She squinted. "Why do you think you should have backed off?"

"I just don't know if I was ready. If you have a breakdown in a relationship, you end up taking the other person with you."

"You think you dragged Hunter down with you after the letter?"

I wiped my face with the back of my hand. Now I was getting confused again. "No. I don't know. When we started dating we stayed at his apartment for four days straight. Skipped our classes and anything else we were supposed to do. Didn't even go outside. I don't think that was good for us."

"Why do you think you retreated like that?"

I thought about it for a moment. "I guess because it took us so long to realize our feelings that we had a lot pent up."

Dr. Schwartz's pen clicked and she wrote something for a moment before speaking. "Do you think he dragged you down?"

I closed my eyes. This was exhausting. "Maybe. His friends made it sound like he has something that's weighing him down too. I don't know. Maybe two messed up people like us can't ever work out."

The pen scratched at the pad a little more before I heard her set it down on the desk and opened my eyes. When I sat up and looked at her, I saw she was staring at me intensely, her lips pursed. Were we finally done for the day? I didn't think I could keep talking about Hunter any more.

"That's all for today, Lorrie. However, before you go, I do think I should ask you to think about whether two people who have dealt with a lot of tragedy in their lives might be better equipped to support each other. There's no right answer to that question, but I think you should stop and consider it before assuming you have the answer already."

I nodded but didn't say anything. Her words might as well have been in another language. It had been a long session, and I was completely and utterly drained. At least I wasn't crying anymore.

"And for what it's worth, I don't think this is the last you've seen of Hunter."

I sighed, staring at her blankly. I didn't want to think about Hunter. I didn't want to think about anything.

Taking the cue that the session was over, I rose shakily onto my feet. After a half-mumbled goodbye, I walked out of her office. I was beyond glad that we were done for the day.

I looked up at the clock in the waiting area and saw there were still ten minutes left before my uncle was due to pick me up. Taking a deep breath, I sat down before realizing this gave me time to clean myself up. I hopped back up and went to the bathroom to clean off my makeup. As I stared at my sunken eyes in the bathroom mirror, I couldn't help but play Dr. Schwartz's words over and over in my head. Was she right? More importantly, did I want her to be right?

Chapter Two
A NEW HOME

Uncle Stewart's charcoal gray Buick sedan had pulled up to the curb when I came out. The sky was gray and sprinkling early April rain, so I was relieved he pulled up rather than parking in the lot and making me walk.

"How was it?" he asked, as soon as I was safely inside. He was wearing a black fleece with his company's logo over a white oxford shirt and pleated chinos. It was his work outfit. He had just gotten off.

"Pretty good," I answered, deciding to simplify things. In reality, my mind was in a million places and I felt like my body had been emptied of tears.

He nodded, pursed his lips, and began driving me the twenty minutes home. My uncle was typically a quiet man, so for him to even ask me about my appointment was a little unusual. He and my aunt were very worried about the way I'd been acting since I got back to their house. I could almost hear my aunt asking me delicately if I might be sleeping too much.

I looked over to see if he was going to say anything more, but his eyes were focused on the road. Uncle Stewart was a salesman who had to do a lot of driving for meetings. Normally he appeared very comfortable behind the wheel, but today he was a little more on edge. His forehead had wrinkled and his grip on the steering wheel was viselike.

I decided to tell him a little more to see if he would relax. "I think Dr. Schwartz actually gave me a lot to think about," I said, trying to sound cheerful.

"Good!" he said, glancing over at me before returning his eyes to the road. I couldn't tell for sure, but it did seem like he relaxed a little bit.

I turned to look out the window. Living with my aunt and uncle had its smothering moments, but I was glad to have somewhere to go. They loved me as one of their own, and I was very thankful for that.

I got back to thinking about what Dr. Schwartz had said. Was I thinking about Hunter the wrong way? I wished I knew what he was dealing with, but he'd refused to tell me. Whatever it was, it was in the past now.

I let out a deep breath. "What's for dinner?" I asked my uncle.

"Not sure what your aunt is cooking," he said. "Probably won't be ready for a while though. She just got home. Joel and Billy had something after school and she was helping out."

He seemed to think for a moment. "If you're hungry we can stop for something on the way home."

I shook my head. "No, that's okay. I don't want to fill up before dinner."

"Are you sure? You haven't been eating much lately."

His words made my stomach sink and I grimaced. My poor aunt and uncle were obsessively worried about me. "Yes, I'm sure," I said. "Eating Aunt Caroline's home cooking will make me feel better than stuffing my face with fast food."

He shrugged. "You're right. Just trying to make sure you don't feel like we're starving you, that's all."

I laughed. My aunt was constantly pushing food on me. Anything so long as it was rich and smelled good. I just hadn't been hungry since I'd gotten back from Studsen. "Not sure how I could ever think that."

My uncle smiled. "Looks like talking to Dr. Schwartz really did help. This is the most lively I've seen you since you came back."

I pursed my lips. "Yeah, maybe. I still have a lot to figure out."

He seemed to consider this. "Okay. Well, your aunt and I just want the best for you. If there's anything we can do to help, we will."

It was my turn to nod. This wasn't the first time we'd had this talk. "Okay. Thank you. I'll let you guys know if there's anything you can do. Right now I think I just need a little space to think."

"Okay. If there's anything else, don't hesitate."

I turned and looked out the window at the passing houses, each one mostly like the last. The roads were still wet, but it looked like the rain had at least stopped. In fact, the sun was even beginning to peek out. I was pretty sure we were getting close to the Perkins house. Or home, I still couldn't decide. I didn't really have a place that felt like home at that moment.

How long was I going to be living in Eltingville with my aunt and uncle? It was wonderful to be able to come back here when I was having a hard time, but I couldn't stay forever. At some point I had to become a self-sustaining adult with a life of my own, even if I never totally got over what happened to my parents.

This was a rut I needed to get out of, and part of getting out was going to be cutting myself free of everything unresolved that had happened in the last few months. There was no point in having yet more baggage dragging me down. Maybe talking to Hunter one more time would be for the best.

I took a deep breath, my heart racing already at the prospect. "Actually there is one thing. I should probably get a new phone soon, so I don't completely lose touch with the friends I made at school."

"Good idea," my uncle said quickly. "Maybe we can go to the store after dinner tonight. If not tonight, tomorrow. Don't want to keep you from your friends."

"Sounds great," I said, leaning back in my chair. "Thanks so much."

A chill ran through my body. Was it too late to work stuff out with Hunter? Probably, but I could at least make sure he was okay. There might even be a chance to find out what had happened the last couple weeks. Maybe I could call him the next day. Or that weekend. Soon, anyway.

We turned onto the street the Perkins lived on. I was feeling pretty hungry, actually. Maybe I would have a tiny snack before dinner. Just some chips or something. Nothing big. I didn't know what the Perkins family usually had for snacks.

"Wonder whose car that is," my uncle said.

I snapped out of my dreams of salty goodness and looked out the window. There was a beat-up old car the size of a small boat parked in front of the Perkins house.

My stomach churned with dread. I knew who it was before we even pulled up.

He was standing at the front door talking with Aunt Caroline, his head down. From the expression on my aunt's face, the conversation looked serious.

It could only be one person.

Chapter Three
HEALTHY

I opened the door and got out of the car shakily. Hunter turned around.

My insides dropped in freefall. I blinked, and an image of the last time I saw him flashed through my mind. He looked better now, but a bandage stretched across the bridge of his nose and there were multiple cuts in various stages of healing on his face. The skin around his left eye was a deep shade of purple.

Under the weight of all the emotion, I had trouble standing up. I leaned against the door of the car to stay upright. What should I say? I wanted to run into his arms and bury my face in his chest and flee the scene all at the same time. How did he find me? Why was he here?

"Hunter . . . "

His name caught in my throat and came out half-mumbled. I tried again to say it more clearly but found I couldn't keep my voice steady. I didn't want to burst into tears. Not now. Not yet.

His glimmering eyes met mine, a boyish smile tinged with sadness crinkling his face. "Hey," he said quietly.

I bit my lip, casting my eyes downward.

Uncle Stewart cleared his throat uncomfortably. "Looks like you kids have a lot to talk about. I'll be inside with your aunt."

He gave a curt nod to Hunter before walking into the house. I watched Uncle Stewart leaving with a mixed feeling of relief and dread. Aunt Caroline gave me a smile and encouraging nod.

Hunter and I would be alone. We were finally getting a chance to talk. Before I left Studsen, I thought that this was what I wanted, but now that the moment was here, I wanted desperately to run away.

I swallowed and took a shuddering breath. Lips trembling, I tried again. "Hunter, I—"

It felt like my throat was swollen, and I just couldn't get the rest of the words out. Warm tears welled in my eyes, streaking down my face.

Hunter took a few long strides and was suddenly in front of me, enveloping me in his scent. His arms wrapped around me tightly and held me to his body.

The familiarity of being in his embrace drove spikes of pain and regret through my heart. I pushed him away gently after a moment and searched his eyes.

Hunter brought the back of his hand up to my face, tenderly smearing away the wetness. "I'm sorry for this," he said, his voice choked with emotion. "I'm sorry I made you so upset. Please give me a chance. I—I know I don't deserve it."

Words started tumbling out of my mouth, tripping over each other. "I'm sorry," I slurred, the tears falling faster. "I'm so sorry . . . I wanted to stay and talk and I went to your place and then I waited but—"

He held on to me tighter and I buried my face into his soft hoodie again.

"I never meant to leave you like that after your fight," I continued. "I failed all my classes and I was confused and I didn't know what to do but you weren't there and then Gary said . . . "

Hunter held me close, rocking me slightly, not saying anything. My tears dampened the fabric of his hoodie, spreading to form a large wet spot. I could feel the warmth of his body seeping through his clothing, enveloping me.

His voice rumbled softly through his chest, like low thunder. "It wasn't your fault. I shoulda been there for you, I shoulda told you what was going on but . . . I just—"

He sighed and shook his head.

I held onto him for a moment longer and then looked up into his face. His eyes were bright, even though his face was battered.

"Can we walk a bit?" he asked.

I nodded, sniffling and still recovering from the shock of seeing him. The pulse pounding through my ears was almost deafening. There were so many questions running through my head, so much I didn't understand.

Why had he come out of the hospital with Ada? Had he been hurt? How come he didn't tell me? Why had Hunter been fighting the day I left Studsen? Was it because of the breakup letter I left him? If it was, then why was he being so sweet to me now?

Hunter grabbed my hand and we walked down the path behind Aunt Caroline's house, which led to a light wooded area. The sensation of his skin against mine jolted through me and almost led to another fresh round of tears. Touching him was a painful reminder of what we had lost, but I didn't want to pull my hand away.

We continued walking slowly in silence for a while until we were deeper into the woods. The mid-afternoon sunlight streamed through the trees, making patterns on the ground. The leaves on the trees were budding fresh for springtime, and there was a chill in the air. It almost reminded me of the area around Lake Teewee where I had first met Hunter.

He looked over at me and smiled sadly. His lips parted as if to say something, but he shook his head and looked away. It was stupid, but my eyes immediately flicked to his lips, wanting to feel them on mine again. I blinked away the stinging in my eyes.

It broke my heart to have him treat me so well after how things between us had ended. I wanted him to yell at me, to blame me, to hate me. At least that would have been easier to understand.

We finally stopped at a clearing. Hunter let go of my hand and sat down on a small rock. I sat down on the larger one opposite him. Our knees were only inches apart, and the slight warmth of his legs against mine made me anxious.

"Gary said you came to the fight," he said. "I guess you saw everything, huh?"

Thinking about the fight was painful. Images of Hunter's broken body falling to the mat flashed through my mind. I closed my eyes and sucked in a deep breath, refusing to let myself cry. "I saw the end of it. Why did you take that fight last minute? Gary said it was my fault."

A tortured mix of emotions contorted his face. "No, it was my fault. I thought I'd lost you and needed to take out my anger. I thought I could take the guy and didn't really care if I couldn't. I wanted to try. Needed to."

My vision blurred as fresh tears came to my eyes. I blinked them away. "I'm sorry I left, Hunter, but I—I just couldn't stay in Studsen anymore."

"I don't blame you for leaving the way you did. After the dumbass way I handled things, I don't blame you at all."

I didn't say anything. Maybe he didn't blame me, but I was at least partially responsible. I let out a deep breath and the air fogged lightly in front of me. Hunter didn't say anything, but I didn't know what else to say either. My fingers tingled with anxiety. I knew he didn't drive to Indiana to take a walk with me. We sat in silence, listening to the sporadic chirping of birds.

After a while he exhaled sharply and shifted on the rock he was perched on. "Listen Lorrie, that day when you saw Ada and I coming outta the hospital, I wasn't trying to avoid you."

I looked away from him, remembering the frustration I had felt that day. "I waited at your place for hours, Hunter."

When I turned back to him, his face looked pained. "I went to look for you and I couldn't find you, so I freaked out," he said, his eyes searching mine. "Then I went over to Gary's to talk about what to do, and we ended up getting wasted."

I shook my head in disbelief. It was so stupid. I was waiting in his apartment for him and he was out looking for me everywhere else. Then, rather than come home, he got drunk with his friend. "Okay, fine, but why were you in the hospital with Ada in the first place? Did something happen to you? Are you—are you okay?"

"Huh? Yeah, I'm fine." Hunter's grey eyes darted to me and then away. His shoulders were tense as he took a deep breath and bent over to pick up a thin twig from the ground. "I mean . . . well, no. Not exactly."

My throat thickened. Not exactly? What did that mean? Hunter played with the twig, drawing lines in the soft peat, still avoiding eye contact. I waited patiently, watching him, while my mind raced through thousands of improbable scenarios.

Hunter snapped the twig in his hand.

"Lorrie, I have MS. Multiple sclerosis. It's a disease . . . It's not curable, but it can be treated, only . . . " he trailed off, a pained grimace on his face.

Ice gripped my stomach and my head felt like it was about to float away. I watched him carefully, waiting for him to say more. My hands involuntarily rose to my mouth. MS? Multiple sclerosis?

Hunter hadn't changed his posture, but suddenly he looked different. I always took comfort in the size of his body, feeling safe in his presence. Now I saw the worry etched on his face, the tired slump in his shoulders and the pain in his eyes. Tattoos and Muscles. Tim. "The Hammer." An MS patient.

Sharp spikes of pain lanced through my chest and I felt my heart breaking for him. This wasn't fair. Hunter didn't deserve this.

"I had no idea," I choked out, hot tears springing uncontrollably from my eyes.

"Hey, don't cry Lorrie. I'm the one who's dying," he said, a lopsided smile trembling on his lips. Typical Hunter. Even now, he had to tell his stupid jokes.

"That's not funny," I shot at him. The smile faded from his face, leaving only the sadness in his eyes.

"Sorry," he mumbled. "Bad joke."

Other than the injuries from his fight, he looked mostly in good health, but how long would it last? I didn't know much, but I was pretty sure multiple sclerosis could be debilitating. It was one of those diseases like Parkinson's that you really didn't want to have. When did he find out? Why hadn't he told me earlier?

"That day you ran into us outside the hospital, I had just gotten discharged. I had a flare-up, but I'm fine now."

It was another revelation that felt like a slap to the face. That was why he had been in the hospital. Waves of guilt washed over me. Hunter had been hospitalized while I was trying to recover from the shock of receiving Marco's letter. I had been upset at Hunter because he wasn't there for me, when in reality, he was struggling with something worse. I swallowed thickly, feeling nauseated.

"When did you get diagnosed?" I asked, wiping the tears that kept falling from my face.

"Sophomore year."

"And Ada knows about it?"

He sighed. "Yeah, we were dating when I found out."

A fresh pang of pain clutched around my heart. He hadn't trusted me enough to tell me, so much that he went to his ex for help. Who else knew about it? Was I the only one in the dark? Is that why everyone else seemed to know what was going on except for me?

"Who else knows?"

"Just Gary."

I pursed my lips. So Gary had been hiding it from me too. "Why didn't you call *me*? I would have gone to the hospital with you!"

"I was afraid—" he paused to take several deep breaths and then started over, "This disease has taken away *everything* from me and when I thought there was nothing left for it to take . . ."

The muscles in his jaw tightened and then relaxed. "I met you."

He took my hand and squeezed it. "I saw that you were dealing with so much pain, so I wanted to be your rock. I didn't want you to pity me and just see me as some sick dying patient!"

Heavy puffs of his warm breath rose from him. His eyes were full and glistening with emotion.

"I wouldn't have . . . " I started to say that I wouldn't have looked at him that way, but my voice trailed off when I realized that was a lie. Just moments ago when he had told me about his condition, that was exactly how I had started to see him.

When I was at school, a lot of people tiptoed around me like I was going to have a breakdown any moment. Hunter was different. He had treated me like I was still a real person, not a pity case. Maybe I was still struggling with how I was coming to terms with Hunter's condition, but I was determined to see through it to the real man underneath.

"Hunter, I understand why you were worried, but you didn't even give me a chance. I told you all of my secrets. Why did you keep this from me? I never would have even left Studsen if I knew!"

My heart pounded in helpless fury at the stupid things we did and could never take back. I was angry at Hunter and I was angry at myself.

He shook his head vigorously. "I wanted to help you with your pain, not add my problems to yours. That's why you had to leave Studsen, isn't it? Because something happened? I woulda never forgave myself if I was the only reason you stayed."

"But *why*? I thought we were supposed to be a team. We were supposed to save each other!"

I stomped my foot, shaking up some of the dirt on the ground. Hunter held his other hand to the side of my face and leaned in until our foreheads were touching. His gray eyes were soft liquid pools I wanted to drown in. "We can still save each other. Just give us a chance."

I let out a choked sob, unable to stand looking at his hopeful expression. His breath blew softly against my face as his chest rose and fell. Hunter was dealing with a horrible disease without a cure, and I was still no closer to moving on from how my parents died. I knew I loved him. I just didn't know if our love was something that could work with everything else in our lives.

"How can we save each other if you won't even ask for help when you need it?" I asked weakly.

He shook his head desperately. "You don't know how sorry I am, Lorrie," he said. He looked up to the sky and took a deep breath. "What we had was something special, and I ruined it. I know I shoulda told you sooner. Knew it then too, I think."

No. Hunter wasn't the only one who ruined it. I was responsible too. I tried to be normal and have a normal life, but I messed it up. Even before everything fell apart, I knew that what was happening between us would lead to disaster. And now that I knew about Hunter's condition, would I even be strong enough to help him deal with it?

Gary's voice broke into my thoughts. *You're no good for each other.*

I turned my head away from Hunter and he let his hand drop. "That's not the only problem. I care about you, and I want you to be okay, but when we were together . . . maybe everything wasn't as perfect as you thought it was."

"What are you talking about?" he asked, concern furrowing his brow.

I pulled my hand away from him. "We stayed in your apartment for days just so we could have more sex! How was that healthy? We were hiding from reality!"

"How many people have had to deal with the things we're going through?" he shot back. "Don't you think we deserved a little break?"

"Not like that! A little break could become a permanent vacation for us. Everyone else around us saw it, but we were so deep into each other that we didn't see what was happening."

His voice rose. "Who did you hear that from? Was it Ada? I swear to God, if she's trying to fuck with you—"

I slapped my hands against my thighs in anger. "No! Stop it! This isn't about Ada or anybody else! It's about us. Don't you see? We could have avoided this mess."

He stared at me for several seconds, breathing hard. "Yeah, I know," he said finally. His eyes moved from my face back to the gray sky. "I fucked it up, but I'm trying to make it right."

I thought about what had happened after I'd received Marco's letter.

"No, it's not just you. It's me too. We're like two people drowning. We weren't careful and got our limbs tangled together and then we both sank to the bottom!"

"Lorrie, it's not like that—"

"Yes it is!" I yelled. "Look at what happened to us. You took a fight and got beaten up right after you came out of the hospital."

"It wasn't your fault," Hunter continued to protest.

"It *was* my fault! And it was your fault too! It was *our* fault!"

My breaths were coming quickly now, almost panting. It looked like my words were slowly sinking in and I could tell he was trying to think about it.

I tried to steady myself. "It's not that I don't care about you, or that I don't want to be with you. I just don't know if we can make it work without hurting each other."

He sighed and ran his hands through his hair, making it messier. "Fine, maybe it was our fault. We got a little too intense. But you know what Lorrie? I've never felt anything like being with you. I know you feel the same way too. That's gotta be something right?"

His looked at me, his eyes expectant and challenging, but I didn't know how to face him. I looked down at my shoes, trying to put into words how I felt.

"I don't know," I said, sighing deeply. Nothing made sense. I was drained and exhausted and I didn't want to argue anymore. When I woke up that morning, I thought I would never see Hunter again. Now, he was here in front of me, had a horrible illness, and wanted to work things out. My temples were pounding and I could barely even think straight.

He took my hand in his. "Please, Lorrie. We can do this."

I massaged my forehead, but it did nothing to ease the pounding pain. I didn't know if what Hunter wanted was possible or not, but we couldn't just keep pushing each other away. If I'd learned anything the past couple months, it was that Hunter and I couldn't be just friends. Keeping each other at arm's length would only lead to more pain. Still, how could we build something healthy together?

Hunter was still looking at me, his face open and hopeful.

Dr. Schwartz thought that we might be good for each other, but our first try at a relationship had ended in disaster. Still, I didn't doubt that he loved me. He wouldn't have come all the way out here if he didn't.

Now that he had confided his secret to me, I couldn't just turn my back on him. Not when he needed me most. How could I give up on Hunter when he refused to give up on us? I didn't know if I was strong enough to help him carry his burdens, but I had to try.

I looked away into the woods for a few moments, trying to think of what to say. I wanted to give Hunter a chance, but I needed to make sure he understood that we couldn't do it the same way again this time.

"I don't want to use each other to hide from our problems," I said finally. "I don't want to keep hiding and running anymore."

I watched him carefully for his reaction.

"We won't," he said. "We'll face them together."

His eyes were open and eager, but I wasn't sure if he really understood what I meant.

"If we're going to save each other, you can't look at me like I'm always the one who needs rescuing," I said. "That's—"

"Lorrie, I—"

I had to get it out now, while I still could. "No! Please let me finish. The reason I left Studsen wasn't because of you, but if you told me the truth, none of this would've happened."

Hunter swallowed, his Adam's apple bobbing up and down. "I'm sorry. No more secrets. I promise."

I stared into his eyes and my heart melted for him. Dealing with his MS had to be so hard. Constantly worrying about his health. The fear that he might be stuck in a hospital bed for the rest of his life . . . or worse. It would have been so easy for him to never see me again after how I ended things, but he decided to drive hours to come here to try to work things out.

"Okay," I said finally.

His face brightened and he threw his arms around my shoulders, hugging me against his massive body.

I leaned into him for a moment before pulling back to look into his eyes. "We have to go slow this time, though. We have a lot of things to think about. All of this . . . all of this is so much for me. I thought I'd never see you again, and now you're here."

My pulse started to speed up. "If we go too fast and don't think about how to make this healthy, we'll make a mess of things, and this time I just know that it'll be worse."

He nodded slowly, squeezing my hand tighter. "We'll go slow, Lorrie."

I hoped that he had the self-control to do what I asked, because I didn't know if *I* had it. His lips were just a few inches away, but I closed my eyes, grateful that he just wanted to hug me for now.

We held onto each other for a few minutes and my headache slowly faded to a dull throb. When I felt like I was back on earth again, the concerns of the wider world started to come back.

"What are you doing about your classes?" I asked him.

"I can miss a few classes. You're more important than that."

I frowned. Hunter was pretty smart, but I didn't like that he was skipping classes. I decided to leave that up to him for now. Still though, I wanted to make sure we were clear. "You can't hurt yourself for me Hunter. Are you going to be okay, you know, after being in the hospital?"

"Yeah, I'm fully recovered now. I even brought my prescriptions, so if I gotta stay a little longer, I'll be fine here. There's motel a few miles away. I'll just crash there for the night."

I nodded and we sat there for a moment, holding each other.

"Listen," he said, "I know you've got a lot to think about, but can I see you tomorrow?"

It had been a long day. Having some time to think about it and talk after a good night's sleep sounded like a positive step to me.

I put my head on his shoulder. "Yeah. I'd like that."

Letting out a deep breath that I hadn't realized that I'd been holding, I wiped my eyes with the sleeve of my shirt. We sat in silence for another few minutes. Dr. Schwartz had been right about Hunter. It wasn't over for us yet.

After a while I realized it was starting to get dark. How long had we been out here? The last time I had been in these woods for too long, Aunt Caroline had called the police because she thought I'd disappeared. That definitely didn't need to happen again.

"Let's head back to the house," I said, standing up and dusting my pants off. "I don't want my aunt to worry about us."

Hunter didn't say much as we walked back to the house so I gave him his space. He seemed thoughtful, which comforted me. If we were going to make it, we needed to be on the same page.

The world had thrown us into the deep end, and we were both just trying to keep our heads above water.

He had rescued me from drowning once, before he even knew me. Now that all of our secrets were in the open, was it even possible for us to save each other?

Even though I was terrified of the fallout if we failed, I was happy we still had a chance.

Chapter Four
AWKWARD

We returned to the driveway by the same path we had walked into the woods, the dim light fading fast in the sky.

When we got to the front of the house where Hunter's car was parked, he turned to me. "Hey, don't be mad, but I have something to show you."

He went to the back of the the beat-up blue car and beckoned me over. I followed him, curious. Then he pointed into the dirty windows of the backseat. I shrugged and peered in, not knowing what to expect. The thin layer of dust on the window made it hard to see anything—especially in the low light—but then I spotted it.

In the backseat was a large cardboard box covered in a blue blanket made of thick wool. A tiny fuzzy tail poked out from underneath.

"Oh my god! Why did you bring them all the way here?"

He shrugged boyishly. "Dunno. I figured you might wanna see your babies."

"Were they okay on the drive over?" I asked, a little worried that the kittens had spent hours in the car.

"Yeah, no problems at all. They mostly just slept."

I shook my head, but even in my exhausted state I had trouble keeping a smile from my face. The little tail poking out wiggled a bit and then disappeared under the blanket.

"Why didn't you just leave them in Studsen and have Gary take care of them?"

"Gary's been pretty busy with his frat, and besides, I figured they're our responsibility. Don't worry, I made sure they were comfortable during the ride."

Judging from the fact that the six little monsters were all asleep at the moment, they must've been just fine.

The front door to the house opened and a splash of light illuminated us. Aunt Caroline stood in the driveway.

"Dinner's ready!" she called. "Hunter, why don't you come in and join us?"

My spine straightened. I'd been ready to say goodbye to Hunter and regroup on my own. We'd just started to work things out, and I didn't relish the prospect of an awkward family dinner before we could spend more time talking alone. Plus, Uncle Stewart could be pretty conservative. I wasn't sure how open he would be to anyone dropping in on the family, never mind someone who looked like Hunter.

Hunter turned quickly to her and stood up straighter himself. "Hi Ms. Perkins," he said. "Lorrie and I just finished talking. I'm sorry I kept her so late."

Aunt Caroline brushed it off. "Oh don't worry about it! Now come inside, so I can fill you up."

I opened my mouth to protest, but decided against it. Spending more time with Hunter would be good, and if my aunt wanted to invite him, she had to figure Uncle Stewart sharing a dinner table with Hunter wouldn't be *too* awkward.

Hunter seemed to consider, then his face screwed up into a sheepish grin. "Well, the thing is, the kittens are actually in the car, and I didn't want to bring them in and mess up your place."

After he said that, it was pretty much a done deal. Aunt Caroline practically squealed. "You brought the kittens? Bring them in! I'm sure the boys would love playing with them."

When my aunt first invited him to dinner I thought she was just being polite, but now I didn't know what was going on. She was being *very* insistent. Hunter looked to me, the question in his eyes. I smiled and nodded.

"Thank you, Ms. Perkins," he said, opening the back door of his car to pick up the box of kittens.

My aunt smiled at me as I walked in after Hunter, but I could already feel tightness building up between my shoulder blades. She was definitely up to something. I just didn't know what that was.

All I could do was hope for the best.

We were seated in the kitchen because the dining room was being redone. It made things pretty cramped with six people, but we managed. Hunter and I had brought the kittens in from the car. Now they were in a box in the corner of the room. Most of them were sleeping, but Taylor and Rampage—the two usual troublemakers—were out of their box and exploring their newest environment.

This could not have been more distracting for my cousins. They were already antsy, being nine and eleven, but the introduction of the kittens took their usual energy to a new level. The high-pitched screams that resulted did nothing to help my nerves.

Hunter, for his part, seemed to be handling everything without missing a beat. He was joking around with my cousins and generally being as charming as I'd ever seen him. Maybe more so. He hadn't struck me as much of the kids type, but apparently, I was wrong.

We sat down to an Aunt Caroline specialty: pork chops and a crunchy sweet potato casserole with a side of green beans. Hunter's eyes got big as she set the plates down in the center of the table.

"Wow, looks like you guys eat well," he said as everyone got situated.

My uncle smiled from his place at the head of the table to my left. "Caroline is quite the cook."

Aunt Caroline took her seat at the other end of the table and we began passing around the food. I went first and passed to my uncle.

"Well I'm thankful to have a family of good eaters," my aunt said. "Hunter, you're a good eater, right?"

Hunter tore his eyes from the food being passed around and faced my aunt. "Yup. I hope I'm not being a burden here. You probably weren't expecting company."

Aunt Caroline shook her head and served Hunter's plate before hers. It was a big helping. "Oh don't worry about that. There's plenty of food to go around and we're happy to have you."

She was in the middle of finally serving herself when her head snapped to her right. "Joel! No feeding the kittens people food! It'll make them sick."

I had no idea how she saw that. She seemed to have eyes in the back of her head. Joel, the guilty party, looked suitably ashamed of himself and went back to picking at the food on his plate with his eyes down. I started eating. The food was delicious, and the more I ate the more I realized how hungry I was.

Uncle Stewart looked undisturbed by the episode. His attention was focused on Hunter. Uncle Stewart eyed him carefully, apparently sizing him up. "Where did you get the kittens, Hunter?"

There was a pause as Hunter chewed his food. "Rescued them," he said once he had swallowed. "They were in a box on the side of the road. I was running to the gym when I saw the box and decided I had to save them. Lorrie was a huge help from the start, actually."

My uncle nodded with a small smile on his face, seemingly amused by that answer. I couldn't get a read on his opinion of Hunter. "Good for you. Did they do that to your face?"

I cringed and put my fork down harder than I meant to, causing it to clink loudly against the plate. This was exactly what I was worried about. How were we going to explain that Hunter got injured in a cage fight? My eyes shot back and forth as I prayed nobody had noticed my clumsiness.

They hadn't, or at least they weren't showing it. Aunt Caroline and Uncle Stewart were focused on Hunter, and the boys were busy with their food. I panicked, trying to come up with an excuse to give my uncle for Hunter's injuries, but I was too exhausted from the day to come up with anything good.

Hunter paused a second, then pointed to his face and laughed. "What, this? No, the kittens aren't that vicious yet. I fell down the stairs in front of my apartment, actually. Trying to carry a coffee table inside. Stupid."

My eyes flew over to my uncle.

He winced theatrically. "Did the table survive?"

Hunter met his gaze without flinching. "It was still in the box. Got it at an IKEA. So yeah, it was fine. A lot better than I was."

"You look like you go to the gym quite a bit," my aunt said, changing the subject.

Hunter looked a little uncomfortable for a moment but smiled eventually. "Yeah, I like to work out."

"Do you play any sports?" Billy asked.

I held my breath. It was doubtful that Uncle Stewart would think of getting knocked out in a cage surrounded by drunken spectators as a sport.

"I used to wrestle in high school," Hunter answered. "Do you play any sports?"

"Baseball and soccer," he said, nodding sagely. "My mom won't let me play football. She says the players hurt their heads too much."

Hunter's eyes shot quickly to me before going back to Billy. "Well, it is a dangerous game," he said diplomatically.

"Yes it is," my aunt said. There was agreement all around and we went back to our food.

We all ate in silence for a couple minutes. The food tasted good, but my mind was elsewhere. I couldn't figure out why Aunt Caroline and Uncle Stewart were questioning Hunter as much as they were. It wasn't quite unfriendly, but something seemed forced.

Suddenly I heard the sink come on, followed by the high-pitched sound of one of the kittens yowling.

"What's that?" I asked.

But Hunter was already out of his seat and rolling up his sleeves to go to the sink. Aunt Caroline followed close behind. Hunter reached in and pulled out a soaking wet Taylor, who looked very displeased at what had just happened.

"I'm sorry," he said to my aunt and uncle. "Do you have a towel or anything I can use to dry her off?"

The boys had gotten up for a better look at the unhappy kitty, who was squirming in Hunter's arms. They were delighted at the excitement. Aunt Caroline handed Hunter a dish towel with an amused look on her face.

"Okay boys, excitement's over. Back to dinner."

"How did she turn on the faucet?" Hunter asked as he dried Taylor off tenderly.

"It's one of those new sinks where you just have to touch the spout and it turns on or off," I answered, finally realizing what had happened. "She must have touched it on somehow."

"We just got it installed," my aunt added, taking her place back at the table. "It's amazing for when you're cooking. Not so much for cats, I guess."

Everyone laughed, including Uncle Stewart. It felt good to laugh at something silly. I was starting to feel more normal again.

After the laughter died down, Uncle Stewart gestured at Hunter's arms as Hunter stood drying Taylor. "I see you have some tattoos."

I swallowed nervously.

Uncle Stewart continued. "Caroline got a tattoo. To each their own, of course, but I have to say I don't really get it. You have those things forever, you know."

His tone didn't seem quite hostile, but it still put me on edge.

Hunter shrugged. "I guess I see it as self-expression. If I wake up in twenty years and hate them, I guess I gotta deal with it then."

Hearing Hunter talk about the future gave me a sick feeling in my stomach. Would he be around in twenty years? Would he be disabled if he was?

No. I couldn't think like that. Treating Hunter like he was a patient just waiting to die was exactly what he was afraid of. I had to be stronger than that for him. Plus, I had no idea if it was even true. Maybe he'd be fine for years.

"Thank you, Hunter," Aunt Caroline said. "Stewart has been asking me about my tattoo every other day since I got it."

I exhaled, relieved my aunt had come to Hunter's rescue.

"That's not quite true," Uncle Stewart said. "I just don't understand what point you're making by getting a tattoo."

Aunt Caroline shook her head. "I swear you're taking this thing as a call for help," she said with a laugh.

My uncle turned to me. "Lorrie, what do you think?"

I looked furtively around the table and took a quick breath. "I think if the most Hunter and Aunt Caroline have to worry about in twenty years is their tattoos, they're in pretty good shape."

Sweat prickled across my skin. I had to keep reminding myself that nothing really bad was happening. I was just being nervous and assuming things that weren't necessarily true. Hunter and I hadn't really had a chance to talk too much about his condition. I made a mental note to ask him more questions about it as soon as we were able to get some alone time.

He shook his head. "I guess I'm on an island here. Boys, no tattoos while you live under my roof. Understand?"

I cracked a smile as the two looked wide-eyed at their father. They hadn't been paying attention to the conversation. The spectacle of the kittens—and especially of Hunter drying off Taylor—was too much to resist.

"I think you'll have to remind them," I said.

He shook his head and we went back to finishing dinner, which by this point was getting lukewarm. I was finally starting to relax. Whatever motives Uncle Stewart and Aunt Caroline had, Hunter seemed to be handling this well. He came back to the table after finishing with Taylor and began eating his dinner quickly.

"So are you staying around town, Hunter?" Uncle Stewart asked.

"I was planning on getting a motel around here, actually. Me and Lorrie are gonna hang out some more before I head back to Studsen."

My uncle nodded. "There's no need to do that. We have room for you here and Caroline and I don't mind having you stay."

I was pretty sure my jaw had just dropped, but I didn't even have time to check before my aunt chimed in. "I think it's going to break the boys' hearts if you leave without letting them play with those kittens just a little more."

Hunter looked back and forth between them, as surprised as I was. "Oh no, I can't do that. I really don't want to be a burden, especially with the kittens."

"Nonsense," my aunt said. "I love cats, and none of us are allergic. I'm sure those little darlings will be no trouble at all. They've already gotten so much bigger!"

Hunter opened his mouth to respond, but Uncle Stewart spoke first. "You good with tools?"

Hunter's mouth closed quickly and then he answered. "Pretty good, yeah. I used to help out with some repairs at my gym."

"Well, how about you stay with us a few days and help us redo the dining room? It's been a slow project and it would help us out a lot. I've been so busy with work and Caroline has to take care of the boys. Besides, it doesn't make sense for you to waste money at a motel when we've got plenty of space here."

Hunter looked back and forth. Both my aunt and uncle were gazing at him expectantly. I was too stunned to speak. He looked to me briefly, but I just shrugged.

"Uh sure, I guess," he said finally. "That sounds great. Thank you very much."

"Perfect," Uncle Stewart said. He smiled and went back to his food.

I was so confused. Why were my aunt and uncle seemingly doing their best to keep Hunter in the house as long as possible? It was so unlike them, especially my uncle.

We all finished up eating and then helped clean up the kitchen. I tried to catch my aunt's eye to see if she could fill me in on why she and my uncle were so eager to have Hunter stay with us, but it was no use. After dinner it was family time, and I couldn't get her alone. I'd have to wait.

The rest of the evening flew by in a blur. It was strange seeing Hunter in the Perkins house after everything that had happened the past few weeks. He looked like he was totally comfortable, and spent most of the evening playing with Joel, Billy, and the kittens. My aunt and uncle seemed happy to have him. I sat on the couch and tried my best to hide my confusion and process everything that had happened today.

When Bones came up to me and meowed at my feet, I picked him up and snuggled him to my face. I was glad Hunter had brought the kittens. They were a fuzzy reminder of our happiest times.

Finally, it was time for bed. Aunt Caroline cleared out the guest bedroom of most of its junk and changed the sheets so Hunter could sleep there. Everyone said their goodnights—my cousins spent a long time with the kittens—and went to bed.

From the moment I said goodnight to Hunter, all I could think about was how I wanted to curl up with him and fall asleep in his arms again. I knew we couldn't though. I hadn't even told him about getting Marco's letter yet and I still hadn't fully wrapped my head around his condition.

I didn't know if it was going to be easier or more difficult to work things out with Hunter staying with us, but I was starting to feel a lot better than I had this morning.

Chapter Five
A NEW MORNING

I couldn't breathe. My chest spasmed in pain as I tried to inhale. My limbs were slow and heavy. Wet. I was underwater. My left ear itched.

The algae green waters churned around me, bubbles blocking my view. Something rough and strong circled around my waist, clutching around me and making me feel safe. *He was going to save me.* I kicked and flailed my arms, reaching up to my savior. To air. To life. But every movement of my limbs just made me sink deeper into the darkness. A fuzzy warmth rubbed against my nose.

I sank deeper. The darkness stretched out into eternity away from me. I floated along for some time before a face came into view.

It was too dark and I couldn't make out the features, but somehow, I knew it was my dad. I blinked and tried to see him more clearly, but I still couldn't picture him. He was too out of focus. His mouth was flapping. It looked like he wanted to say something to me, but I couldn't hear it. Reaching forward, I tried to swim towards his voice, but it faded away.

When I turned, another face appeared suddenly in front of me. The eyes were wide and crazed, lolling around in the sockets, his grin frozen on his face.

Marco.

I could taste bile rising at the back of my throat. Panic seized my chest and I let out a wordless scream.

I woke up in a sweaty tangle of sheets.

I'm okay.

A high-pitched meow came from the left side of my bed, and I cracked my eyes open to take a look. The brown fur and heart-shaped spot on its back immediately told me it was Taylor.

I'm okay, Marco isn't here.

Groaning, I pushed myself up against the headboard as Taylor climbed over the mountain of sheets and into my lap.

I'm okay, Marco's in prison far away. He can't hurt me anymore.

I thought about Dr. Schwartz's advice regarding Marco. Should I write him a letter to ask why he killed my mom? What would he say? Would he really tell me just because I asked? Is that all I needed to banish him from my dreams?

I shook my head and tried to focus on the present. I could deal with that later. Right now I had an adorable kitten who wanted some attention.

Of course it had to be Taylor waking me up. She was such a trouble-maker. I was glad she had woken me up, though. This time. I rubbed her back gently, while she kneaded the sheets on my lap, trying to find a comfortable spot.

Her gentle purring helped to slow down the erratic beating of my heart. I sucked in a few deep breaths to calm myself down and get Marco's face out of my mind. I tried to recall my father's face, but all I saw was the fuzzy, out-of-focus image from my dream.

When I turned to the clock I saw that it was eight. Yesterday, I had slept in until one in the afternoon before going to see Dr. Schwartz. So much had happened in the span of a day; I was actually feeling a lot better. I didn't know if it was because of the therapy session, or the fact that Hunter and I had finally had a chance to talk, but I liked it.

Whatever the reason, I wasn't about to let a stupid dream ruin my mood.

I reassured myself that I knew what my father's face looked like. He'd always had dark curly hair that fell across his forehead. Sometimes his hair would get into his eyes and he'd brush it away with a wave of his hand. Were his eyes black or dark brown? No, no they were definitely black. Damnit, the dream was bothering me more than it should.

I took a shower and threw on a pair of sweatpants and an old sweater before heading downstairs to the kitchen. On my way there, I passed by Rampage and Frida chasing each other in the hallway.

The savory aroma of bacon reached my nose before I even got to the kitchen, and my stomach rumbled loudly. Aunt Caroline must have made breakfast already. I smiled at the thought of my aunt's delicious, calorie-laden breakfasts. They would be the perfect way to get my mind off of the dream.

When I got to the kitchen I was surprised to see that it was not my aunt, but Hunter at the stove. He was wearing a white t-shirt, his biceps bulging tightly against the sleeves. His cute butt filled up the jeans he was wearing. I smiled to myself guiltily. I guess I could still enjoy that part of Hunter.

Aunt Caroline was sitting at the kitchen table, sipping a cup of coffee.

She beamed at me when she saw me, her eyes twinkling. "Good morning, Lorrie. *Hunter* just made us and the boys breakfast. How are you feeling?"

Hunter turned around and gave me a quick smile. It was still so surreal to see him standing in Aunt

Caroline's kitchen. A concerned look flashed across his face for a second and he turned back to the stove. It seemed like we both wanted a chance to talk alone soon.

"I'm okay," I said. "I see the kittens have taken no time to get adjusted to the house."

Aunt Caroline let out a hearty laugh, "You have no idea. Your uncle was quite surprised to find a fuzzball next to his face this morning! Which one is it, the one with the spot on his back?"

I smiled with her. "That must've been Taylor, she woke me up too. Did Uncle Stewart go off to work already?"

She nodded. "Mmhm, just a few minutes ago."

Hunter put a plate in front of me, with scrambled eggs and slices of bacon. My stomach grumbled its approval loudly.

"Breakfast's served," he said, with a small wink just for me.

Then he turned to my aunt. "Would you like some more food, Ms. Perkins?"

She waved him off, patting her stomach for emphasis. "I'm way too full. Please, have the rest yourself."

Hunter shrugged and plated himself a mountain of food. I couldn't help but smile when I noticed what he was wearing over his t-shirt. I hadn't noticed it earlier when his back was turned, but now it was hard not to laugh at his tattooed arms poking out of Aunt Caroline's frilly apron. I raised an eyebrow at him.

Hunter joined us at the table and looked at me confused for a second before his eyes lit up in realization. "Oh yeah, your aunt insisted that I wear it. She didn't want me messing up my clothes."

I shook my head slowly in disbelief. It was quite the amusing image.

My aunt chimed in. "Hunter even drove out this morning to get some eggs when we ran out. Isn't he the sweetest thing?"

I looked to Hunter, only to see his cheeks stuffed full of food. He chewed and gulped it all down first. "Aw, it's no big deal, Mrs. Perkins. You're letting me stay here, it's the least I could do."

He was certainly making a good impression on my aunt. That gave me one less thing to worry about. Hopefully he was doing the same with Uncle Stewart.

Hunter seemed to want to talk, but he didn't say anything with my aunt there. We ate in silence for a while, as Aunt Caroline sat there sipping her coffee at the table with us.

A little while later, the phone rang. Aunt Caroline put her mug down and walked over to the other side of the kitchen.

"Hello?" she said and then paused. "Oh of course! Yes, she's right here!"

My aunt turned to me. "It's Daniela, she wants to talk to you."

Daniela and I hadn't spoken since a couple of days after I got to my aunt's place. I had filled her in on the whole fiasco with Hunter's fight, but she didn't know that Hunter had come all the way to Indiana to try to patch things up with me.

I had just barely picked up the phone when Daniela voice came through *loud* and clear. "Oh my god, Lorrie. Did he show? Is he there right now?"

I winced and held the phone an inch away from my ear.

"What? Who?" I asked.

"Who?! Are you kidding me? Who else? *Hunter!*"

I looked at him, hoping that he couldn't hear Daniela's voice from across the kitchen, but he was chatting with my aunt.

"Yeah, he's here. Why am I starting to get the impression that I'm always the last person to get the full story?"

"Two days ago he came to find me. At first I was ready to kick his ass for you, but then he kept saying how sorry he was and how he wanted to fix things up. He seemed sincere, so I gave him your aunt's address. He said he was going to surprise you and made me *promise* to not call you until today."

Another piece of the puzzle clicked into place. So that's how Hunter had found me. I looked over at him again. I was happy to see that he had finally taken the apron off, folded it neatly, and placed it on an empty seat.

"Lorrie, don't leave me hanging! Should I have kicked him to the curb? He was practically delirious when he came to me and I thought you said you tried to talk to him but couldn't and—"

I sighed. "It's fine."

"Are you okay? Did I make a mistake telling him where you are? Because I swear, if that guy hurts you again . . . "

I looked over at my aunt and Hunter. They were still deep in conversation.

"I'm feeling better Daniela, a lot better. Everything isn't perfect yet, but we're working things out. Um . . . Can I talk to you later? I'll tell you everything, I promise."

I didn't exactly want to be airing all of this dirty laundry with Aunt Caroline and Hunter sitting right there in the kitchen with me.

"Okay," she said. "Pinky swear."

I nodded, even though I knew she couldn't see me. "Pinky swear. Thanks for checking up on me."

"Bye girl, take care of yourself."

When I rejoined Hunter and my aunt at the table, they were talking about tattoos. Hunter's plate of food was completely empty already, and I couldn't help but smile to myself. Aunt Caroline was right: he could *eat*.

I worked at my own breakfast slowly and zoned out while they talked. After we were done, Hunter grabbed both of our plates and washed them in the sink.

"Ms. Perkins, I'm gonna go work on the dining room floor if that's alright," he said. "I'll chat with you and Lorrie later."

He looked at me as he said my name. Yes, that would be nice. There was still a lot for us to talk about, but it would have to wait.

"Of course dear," my aunt replied. "Thanks for cleaning up."

He left for his home improvement duties, leaving me and my aunt at the kitchen table. Even if I had to wait to continue my talk with Hunter, I *was* finally alone with my aunt. Maybe I could finally get some answers from her at least.

"Aunt Caroline," I started, "I'm starting to wonder why you and Uncle Stewart are being so nice to Hunter."

She looked at me innocently. "What are you talking about?"

"Come on, why did you invite him to stay over with us? It's not that I don't like it but I just don't get it."

My aunt squinted and smiled bemusedly to herself. "Lorrie, I remember how everything was going between you and Hunter when you were still at Arrowhart. With you taking another leave from school and everything, your uncle and I think it would be good for you if you have something stable in your life."

I looked at her but didn't say anything. Stable? Me and Hunter?

"We want you to be happy Lorrie," she added. "Whatever it takes."

I guess it did make me feel better to have Hunter around, even with everything that had happened between us. He could have just stayed in a motel and visited me, but maybe it was better this way. My aunt and uncle must've been really worried about me if they were willing to go to such lengths for my happiness. Aunt Caroline might have liked having Hunter around, but I had my doubts about how Uncle Stewart felt about it.

My eyes wandered to the wall next to the kitchen table. It was covered in photos of the Perkins family. The two boys opening up Christmas presents. My aunt and uncle on their wedding day, smiling and happy. There was even a picture of me when I was just a baby, sitting in front of a coloring book.

There were no pictures of my dad, though.

"Why don't you have any pictures of my dad up?" I asked.

My aunt froze mid-sip for a split second, but continued to drink from her mug. I shifted in my seat, suddenly uncomfortable. Though we had talked about my mother's death, Aunt Caroline and I almost never spoke about my dad's suicide.

She was quietly staring into her cup so I didn't say anything. Maybe I shouldn't have brought it up.

"No reason, really," she said. "We took the pictures down when we were redoing the kitchen and I guess I must've forgotten to put those back up."

It seemed like a strange reason, but I didn't want to keep talking about it. What would my dad have thought? Would he be sad that we had forgotten him? Even though I knew it was stupid, I was a little worried that I might forget what his face looked like. My dream had scared me, however silly that seemed.

"Can I see them?"

She frowned for a split second before answering. "Of course. They're all in that room at back of the basement with the rest of your father's stuff."

"Thanks," I said. "I think I'll go find them."

I got up from the table. Aunt Caroline looked thoughtful, but just nodded.

I wasn't sure what I was looking for, and maybe it was a bad idea to open old wounds, but then again, didn't I tell Hunter that we couldn't keep running from our problems? Now was as good of a time to face the past as any.

Chapter Six
MEMORIES

I walked downstairs, flicked on the lights, and surveyed my surroundings. My aunt and uncle treated the basement mostly as a place for storage, and it showed. Cardboard boxes lined much of the space against the walls, and my cousins toys were scattered everywhere. Keeping my eyes on the ground, I weaved my way around Hot Wheels and Legos to the back room. I wanted to see my dad's face again.

I walked through the room's door and flicked on the lights. It was even more crowded than the rest of the basement. The room was small and contained nothing but boxes of my dad's things. An L-shaped path to the back right corner from where the door was hugging the left wall was the only thing that made the room somewhat navigable.

I took a deep breath and pulled the lid off the box closest to my feet.

Sitting on top of some binders were several drawings I had made as a child. I put the lid down, picked up the delicate stack of yellowing paper and began flipping through.

Each of them was a colored pencil drawing of three people—a mommy, a daddy, and a little girl—in various settings. Several were in front of a house, one was in a park, another was on a beach. One of them even had a dog, which was a wish I'd had as a kid that had never been fulfilled. They were all drawn by a happy little girl from a happy family.

As I stood there, flipping through some of my earliest art work, I began to shake. That little girl was gone. I was never going to feel the things I had felt when I was making those drawings ever again. The security and innocence I had felt in those days had been taken from me.

Tears formed in my eyes and beaded down my cheeks. I wiped them away with my sleeve and put the drawings back into their box so I could keep looking for pictures of my dad.

After sifting through several boxes I finally came to one with pictures in the back corner of the room. I shakily picked up a thick stack and began to flip through them.

The first few were pictures of my aunt and uncle, but then I saw it. My eyes fell on an image of a college-aged man wearing a mustard-colored button down shirt and tan chinos. His dark, curly hair sat on his head youthfully, and he was clean-shaven. It was my father smiling happily for the camera, though I could barely recognize his boyish face. The picture had been taken well before I was born.

My lips turned briefly up then down, and I looked around the room, waiting for tears to come. To my surprise, they didn't. It was just like when I read his suicide letter. I felt like I should cry because that's what people did, but when it came to my dad I just couldn't.

After a while, I returned to the picture. There he was, just as alive as I was now. Just as young. Now he was gone, and worse, he had taken his own life. I thought of his letter again.

I just can't, Lorrie.

I bit my lip hard, but still no tears came.

With a deep breath, I flipped to the next picture and felt a wave of nausea. It was a picture of my family not very different from the colored pencil drawings I had seen earlier. My parents had taken me to Lincoln Park in Chicago. Lake Michigan was in the background, and standing in front of it was my dad, a little older now and with shorter hair, his arm around my mom. Then there was me—standing not even up to my dad's waist—with a giant stick of pink cotton candy and a toothy smile.

We all looked happy, but my parents would get divorced ten years later, and then everything else would happen.

Why? Why had Marco killed my mom? Why did all of this have to happen?

Tears finally came. First some large beads in my eyes, then one quiet sob followed another as I stood there feeling stupid for coming down to the basement and doing this to myself.

I wiped my eyes with my sleeve and looked at the picture again. My mom—her chestnut hair in a perfect nineties perm—looked a lot like I did now. Minus the perm, of course. I tried to imagine having a child in the next few years and couldn't do it.

It was hard to picture my future at all.

A noise came from outside the room, and then I heard footsteps. I quickly rubbed my eyes, hoping to get rid of as much evidence of crying as possible, and held my breath.

It was Hunter. He stopped in the doorway and seemed to evaluate what was going on. We locked eyes. "There you are," he said. "I looked all over the house."

My vision began blurring again with fresh tears and he made his way through the room's path until he was next to me. I held the photographs to my chest and buried my face in his hoodie. He put his arms around me and held me close.

We stood embraced together in silence. Being close to his warmth felt reassuring and I was glad that he was here with me.

After I'd finally composed myself, I pulled away and faced him. He waited patiently for me to speak.

I took a deep breath and wiped my eyes once more. "I came down here to look for pictures of my dad," I said, my voice mostly steady.

Hunter motioned toward the pictures in my hand. "Did you find any?"

As I began to answer a sob seized my chest and choked the words away from my throat. My vision went blurry again. I held the picture of my family in the park for him to see.

He put a hand on my shoulder and I leaned into him, trying to stop my tears. Just when I thought I was calming down, a fresh wave of emotion overtook me. I tried hard to steady myself.

Hunter pulled me closer into his chest and held the hand containing my family picture up for a better view. "Wow," he said. "Is that you?"

I nodded. "And my parents," I added weakly. "Back when they were together. They got married young, then got divorced when I was a freshman in high school."

Then they were taken from me for no reason at all. I whimpered softly and I buried my face into Hunter again.

He ran his hand through my hair and held me, saying nothing. After a few seconds I calmed down.

"Do you remember when this was taken?" he asked.

"I think so, but I'm not sure if I *really* remember it or just *remember* remembering it. We were at a park in

Chicago, where I grew up. I guess it's been so long that it seems like a story now."

He squeezed my shoulder. "I think that makes sense."

"I don't know," I said. "Everything just feels not real right now. With all the stuff that's happened the last couple weeks, I mean."

"Yeah. Lorrie, I can't tell you how sorry I am about the way—"

"It's not that!" I interrupted, more loudly than I had meant to.

Hunter stopped cold as though I had hit him, but said nothing. I took a deep breath and gathered myself. The frustration that had been simmering since I got Marco's letter was getting the better of me.

"I'm sorry. I just meant that it's not just the stuff that's happened between us that makes everything feel strange right now."

He stayed silent and looked at me expectantly. My stomach churned as I thought about the letter Marco sent me. Having to talk about it made me so angry.

"I mean, the reason I left really wasn't you," I said, trying to keep my voice steady this time. "Something else happened."

I looked at the picture of my parents while Hunter stayed quiet.

"I got a letter from my stepfather," I said firmly. My heart thumped rapidly in my ears.

Hunter took a minute to process what I'd just said, then his eyes widened. "Wait, you mean . . ."

I nodded and then broke down, hugging his torso with both arms until I left another wet spot on his sweatshirt wet with my tears.

He brought me in closer. "Shit. I'm sorry, Lorrie. I shoulda been there for you when that happened."

I shook my head, pulled away, and took a deep breath. "It's okay, you had a pretty good reason to be missing. I should have called you when I got the letter rather than a few days later."

His face slowly hardened. "What kinda sick bastard is this guy, anyway? Why did he send you the letter? How did he send it?"

"I don't know how it got through, but the letter just asked for me to write him back. He even had the nerve to ask for forgiveness and tell me he loved me."

"Did you write him back?"

"No. I just went kind of numb after I got that letter. The whole thing's a blur."

I considered whether to talk to him about my therapist's suggestion to write him back, but I hadn't even decided myself.

"And that's when you had your exams and stuff, right?"

I nodded.

He hugged me again. "I'm so sorry Lorrie. I shoulda been there for you. I coulda helped you."

"It's okay. We both could have done things differently. I should've reached out for help sooner."

Hunter frowned and then took my free hand in his. "Lorrie, you're never gonna have to reach very far because I'm gonna be right there by your side. If I have to save you from a freezing lake, I'll jump in. If I have to follow you to the ends of the earth, I'll find a way. If I have to crawl on the ground to be by your side, I'll crawl to you until I'm next to you. There's *nothing* that will stop me from being there for you, Lorrie. Not my MS, not anything."

The intensity with which he held my hand and said the words he said startled me. When I looked up into his gray eyes I not only knew he meant it, but that I wanted him to mean it. Desperately.

"Hunter," I whispered, tears emerging from my eyes and trailing down my face.

We stood chest to chest. He took his hand from mine and touched my face lightly, wiping away my tears. His touch set my body aflame. My breaths shortened as I froze in my place.

His hand came under my chin and tipped my head up toward his. He touched his lips to mine, tentatively at first then firmly, his warm mouth sealing against my lips with a desire so strong it made me tremble. I hugged my arms tighter around him, pressing my body against his as our tongues played softly.

It was over before I was ready. One of my hands went from his back up to grip his short hair. I tried to pull him back down toward me, but he resisted.

"Lorrie," he moaned. "You said we can't go too fast."

My eyebrows shot up and my eyes opened wide. "You don't want to kiss me?"

"Of course I want to kiss you, I just don't want to mess things up between us again."

Part of me wondered if he had a point, but when I looked into his eyes I realized this was just where I wanted to be. I loved kissing him, and there was nothing wrong with it. If Hunter hadn't come all this way to find me, I'd probably still be totally lost right now.

"Hun, I really appreciate you listening to what I said yesterday. But I don't think it's going to hurt if you kiss me again, okay?"

He paused a second, then his hands flew down to my butt and he hoisted me up quickly, his mouth crashing against mine. I gasped and then smiled against his lips, kissing him back. This was more like we were. This was okay.

This time I was the one to break off the kiss, though I was still smiling. "Worried?"

He made a show of considering my question. "Not really."

He started leaning back in for another kiss.

"Lorrie?" my aunt called.

It sounded like she was downstairs. I tapped Hunter's shoulders and he put me down hurriedly. We both straightened our clothes and I flattened out the pictures still in my hand as best I could.

She appeared in the doorway a few seconds later. "Oh, there you are Hunter. Are you two alright?"

"I was just showing Hunter some pictures of my dad," I said quickly.

Her lips made a thin line and she nodded. "Okay. Well, don't stay too long."

"We were just coming up," Hunter said. "Plenty of work to do today."

Aunt Caroline smiled and then turned to go back upstairs without a word. Hunter gave my shoulder a quick squeeze and we made eye contact. His look was apologetic. I shrugged and nodded my understanding as he walked around the boxes in the room and out the door.

When I was alone again, I looked down at the picture in my hand, the feeling of Hunter's lips still fresh on my own. My dad was gone, but that didn't mean I had to forget him.

I decided to continue flipping through the pictures of him in my room. Stack in hand, I left the storage area and followed Hunter and my aunt upstairs.

Chapter Seven
MOVING ON

When I came upstairs I found Aunt Caroline at the kitchen table writing out a list of groceries she had to get for the week. Judging by the noise, Hunter was already back at work in the dining room.

She looked up from her list as I came into the room. "So did you find some pictures of your father?"

I stood for a moment and processed her question before flipping to the first picture I found of my dad and handing it to her.

She took it hesitantly, looked at it, and put her hand to her mouth. "Oh my goodness, his hair! Bill had such beautiful hair when he was young."

I didn't know what to do, so I did nothing. How long had those pictures been down there?

"That is such a nice picture. What are you going to do with it?" she asked.

"I don't know. I just wanted to bring it to my room for now, I guess."

She tore her eyes away from the photo in her hand. "Okay. What are your plans for the day?"

"For now I was just going to keep flipping through these in my room. It would be nice to have some pictures of him upstairs. Maybe I could go get some frames later at Target or something."

She winced, but quickly got her expression back to neutral and handed me the picture. I took it from her and went up to my room, thinking about her reaction to my idea of getting some pictures of my dad in the house.

Once I was in my room, I plopped onto my bed, lay on my back on top of the off-white comforter, and began sifting through the pictures.

They didn't seem to be in any chronological order. I was in many of them, but there were also several with my dad's cousins and other people I only remember seeing a handful of times at family reunions. All in all, I'd grabbed about twenty pictures.

The picture that stuck out to me was toward the very back. It was a shot of my mom and dad on a tropical beach. They both looked like they might still be in college. The picture had definitely been taken before I was born.

Seeing the way my parents were lovingly embraced made me think of my relationship with Hunter. Kissing him again had been a high and I definitely felt lucky that he had come after me. There was no doubt in my mind we needed each other.

Still, there was a lot for us to overcome. For one, I was worried that this felt too much like a honeymoon period between us and too little like reality. I had no idea what was going on in my life. I couldn't stay at my aunt and uncle's house forever.

Then there was Hunter. Anytime I thought about his future, it was hard not to jump to his MS. No matter how brave he was about it, it was still scary. I had almost no idea what it even was. All I knew was that it had something to do with his nerves or his brain and that it was bad and incurable. Even beyond his disease, I wasn't sure he had any more idea what he was doing with his life than I did.

Plus, I was still dealing with what happened to my parents. Marco's letter had removed the scab from an awful wound. I was trying to move on from their deaths and make some headway into figuring out my future, but every setback made it that much harder.

Maybe my therapist was right and I should write him. The more I thought about it, the more plausible it sounded. What was the worst that could happen? If I got some answers, maybe it would be easier for Hunter and I to build a healthy relationship together. I could be free from the past.

I decided to go for it. Since I'd thrown away the letter Marco wrote me, I had to look up where to address my letter back to him on the Cook County Penal System website. That done, I found a piece of paper and a pen, went to my desk, and scratched something out.

> *Marco,*
>
> *I have been doing my best to recover. One thing has continued to bother me, and you could help with that.*
>
> *Why did you kill my mother?*
>
> *It would help me greatly if I could understand the reason it happened, and maybe it would help you too.*
>
> *Sincerely,*
> *Lorrie*

I looked over the letter again. It asked the question without being too intimate. It definitely didn't make it look like I'd forgiven him, but it was something. Kind of like a business letter or something. I didn't have high hopes, but there was a chance he would read it and have some remorse.

I put it into its envelope and sealed it in. After Aunt Caroline's reaction to Marco's letter, I decided not to talk to her about sending it. I could sneak a stamp at some point and put it in the mail.

Once I was done, I put the envelope into a notebook and left it on my desk. After hopping back on my bed, I began to flip through the pictures again.

My aunt came to my door and knocked twenty minutes later.

"Can I come in?" she asked.

I sat up straighter in bed, glancing briefly at my desk. The envelope was well hidden. "Sure."

She walked into the room and took a seat at the foot of my bed. "Did you find any other good pictures?" she asked.

I picked up the stack and began flipping through them again. I came to a photo of me with my aunt, uncle, and dad taken at a family gathering. Both me and my aunt had our hair up with a scrunchie. "Yeah," I said. "I'm not so sure the scrunchie was a good look though."

I handed her the picture with a smile. She took it and laughed to herself. "Those things really were terrible. God, look at us all. So young. I need to show this to your uncle."

I nodded, and we sat in silence. Finally, I got the nerve to ask the question that had been on my mind all morning. "So what's the real reason you don't have any pictures of my dad up?"

She pursed her lips and looked away for a second. Her face was set in stone by the time she looked back. "When your father . . . when Bill did what he did, I was angry. I couldn't believe he would leave his family behind like that. It's just . . . not what people do."

I had to bite my tongue, but I kept silent.

She looked back at the picture. "As a family, you have to stay together. Through anything. Even if it's terrible, like what happened with your poor mother. Everyone needs to be an anchor for everyone else."

A tear fell from her eye, but she continued talking with a steady voice. "Anyway, I'm glad you brought the pictures up. Even if he did what he did, he's still a part of the family, and we can't abandon him or his memory. He doesn't deserve that."

She paused a moment and pressed her lips together.

"When I think about it, I wish I had done more to reach out to him. He was always an obsessively focused person. In the end I guess it killed him—and it was bad for his marriage, of course—but he did accomplish an awful lot."

Tears began threatening to come from my eyes, but I fought them back as well as I could. I didn't want my aunt to stop talking, even if the mention of my parents' marriage made me upset.

"He was always focused on something," she said with a sigh. She looked back at the picture again. "Maybe something positive to focus on would help you move on too."

"Yeah, maybe," I said, not completely convinced.

She smiled. "I'm going to go downstairs and start on lunch. That boy Hunter eats like a horse. Will you be coming down?"

"Yeah, I'll be down in a minute."

She nodded and walked out. I watched her go and thought about what she'd said.

I threw the covers off and swung my feet around to get out of bed. Everyone in a family needed to be an anchor for everyone else. Had my family been like that?

Probably not. But the Perkins family was welcoming me in and they were family too. Maybe I wasn't pulling my weight yet, but I could work on it.

What about Hunter? I had felt like he was my anchor, but after the last few weeks maybe I needed to be more careful about that. He needed me to be his anchor as much as I needed him. We had certainly made progress, but we weren't fully there yet.

I looked at my desk, where I had hidden the letter to Marco. Maybe if I could get some answers about why everything had happened, I could be a better anchor for Hunter too.

Chapter Eight

HELP

I snuck a stamp from the kitchen drawer my aunt kept them in and sent the letter off the next morning. Before I was ready, it was Saturday evening. Hunter had spent most of the past two days working on the dining room. Even though we hadn't talked alone since he'd found me in the basement, his presence in the house was comforting.

I helped my aunt with the dishes after dinner while Hunter read to the kids in the living room. From the sound of it, there was little actual reading being done, and a whole lot of chasing the kittens.

"Sounds like the boys are having fun," I said.

My aunt let out a hearty laugh. "Having Hunter around is like having an older brother for them to play with. They haven't had this much fun since I can remember."

I giggled. Hunter was just like a big boy, in his own way. It wasn't surprising my cousins got along with him so well.

After a few minutes of raucous laughter in the living room, the noise in the living room died down. Aunt Caroline raised an eyebrow at me. "Do you hear that?"

"What? They've finally quieted down."

"That's the sound of two boys about to raise some trouble. I'm going to go check in on them, can you finish up for me?"

I nodded and started stacking the plates into the drying rack. Hopefully my cousins weren't getting into *too* much trouble.

As I was drying my hands, Hunter walked into the kitchen. I smiled at him when he came in, noticing his messy hair. One of the kittens had probably been sitting on his head just seconds before.

"Hey," he said.

"Hey yourself. Thanks for playing with Joel and Billy. I think they really look up to you."

He laughed. "I'm hardly somebody they should look up to."

"I don't know about that," I said, frowning. "What's going on in there, anyway? Aunt Caroline thought you boys were getting into trouble."

"Ah, nothing. We finished the book. Or I did, anyway. Right now I think they're trying to coax Frida out of her hiding spot."

"Maybe we can help," I said. I started to walk towards the living room, but stopped when Hunter didn't follow me.

His eyes darted to me for a moment before he looked aside. "What? Oh, uh . . . yeah."

I felt my muscles go tense. Something was up.

"What's going on? Are the kittens okay?"

"Yeah, yeah. Nothing like that. Can we—" He stopped and tried again. "Can we talk?"

"Of course!" I answered, a little more cheerfully than I intended. He was acting weird and it was making me nervous.

"Let's go to the guest room," he said. He grabbed my hand and led me down the hall.

My pulse pounded in my ears. What did he want to tell me that he didn't want anyone else overhearing?

After I stepped through, he locked the guest room door, his shoulders hunched over and tense. His face was grim and he didn't say anything. I didn't know why, but my eyes were starting to sting. The past few days with Hunter had been wonderful, but I knew it couldn't last forever.

Did he need to go back to Studsen? He couldn't just skip all of his classes, no matter how smart he was. Even so, I wasn't quite ready for him to leave yet.

Hunter cleared his throat, breaking into my thoughts.

"Uh . . . so, I know we didn't talk about this a lot, but . . . "

"What is it? What's wrong?" I asked, my chest tight with anxiety.

"My MS . . ."

My heart raced. "Oh my god. Is it getting worse? I thought—"

"No!" he yelled.

I flinched at his tone and took a step back. I hadn't expected such a strong reaction from him.

He shook his head slowly. "No," he said, more softly this time. "It's not like that. I'm fine."

"It's not? You're okay?"

"Yeah."

First I felt relieved, but then I noticed the look on Hunter's face. His eyes were downcast and he shook his head. "Listen, I can't stand you thinking that I'm gonna die any second. That kills me."

"I'm sorry. I just . . . "

I knew Hunter was right. Even though it was too late, I wished I could take my words back. Why was he always able to be so strong for me but I kept messing it up? He was trying to tell me something important, and the only thing I could think about was my own irrational fear. I was treating him the same way everyone else did when they found about about his MS. I had hurt him.

"It's okay," he said, letting out a heavy sigh.

I swallowed the lump in my throat. I felt like I owed him an explanation.

"I know how important this is to you, but this is just all so new to me. I'm—I'm scared."

His gray eyes searched my face with an intense focus. Then he nodded, his jaw working slowly. "I know you're trying. Don't be scared. Sometimes when you're in a fight being afraid of getting hit is worse than the hit itself."

I nodded, my lips trembling. He grabbed my shoulders and held me to him tightly. I rested my face on his shoulder, inhaling his scent. Just being close to him was making me calmer. Whatever Hunter wanted to tell me, I was ready for it. There was no reason to be afraid. After a few more moments of taking deep, shuddering breaths, I felt more composed again and pulled away.

"What did you want to tell me?" I asked, wiping the moisture from my eyes.

Hunter walked over to the small gym bag he had brought. He pulled out a small black pouch and sat down on the bed with a deep breath. His fists clenched and released. "Can we sit down?"

I followed him over to the bed, not taking my eyes off of the pouch. What was in it that would make him react this way? I put my arm around his shoulders and felt his muscles knotted and tight. His back rose and fell with his breathing. We sat there for a few moments. I waited for him to get ready for whatever he was about to tell me, my pulse pounding in my ears.

"I wanna show you something," he said finally.

I nodded, trying to keep my mind clear.

Hunter unzipped the pouch and opened it on his leg. There was a syringe and a small vial of amber liquid. The curved glass and cruel metal of the syringe made it look dangerous. I held my breath. Thousands of questions popped through the haze of my mind and threatened to spill out of my mouth, but I was determined not to mess it up again.

Whatever this was about, Hunter had chosen to share it with me. The least I could do was be patient and let him take it at his own pace.

"Lorrie, this is my . . ." his voice cracked.

I took his hand in mine, squeezing his calloused fingers in encouragement. His eyes darted around my face.

He sucked in a deep breath before continuing. "This is my MS treatment. I gotta inject it every two weeks. Tonight's the night."

I stared at the syringe kit in his pouch for a while, trying to steady my breathing. I could tell that he was studying my reaction carefully so I tried to keep my face neutral, but my heart was in my throat.

Even after he had told me about his condition, it didn't feel real to me. Hunter still seemed like he was mostly fine, except for the injuries he got from the fight. But now, with his treatment right in front of me, it was suddenly very, very real.

Hunter cleared his throat. "Usually, I get the shots at the health center on campus, but I gotta do them myself tonight."

I couldn't think of what to say. I knew that he was showing me this for a reason, but I didn't want to say something stupid like I had earlier. Even though I could feel his body's warmth, the silence between us expanded until it felt like we were miles apart.

"Is—"

"Lor—"

We both started talking at once, and then stopped. Neither of us said anything for a few seconds, lost in our own thoughts.

Hunter spoke first. "Sorry, you go first."

I took a deep breath so it wouldn't feel like I was suffocating. If I didn't understand much about Hunter's condition, maybe the best thing to do was to just ask him about it.

"Will it make you better?"

He shook his head. "It just prevents the episodes from getting worse."

It was a stupid question and I kicked myself mentally for even asking it. He had said that there was no cure.

I pointed to the pouch. "Does it hurt? I mean, you know, the needle."

His eyebrows furrowed as he considered it for a second.

"Not as much as being in a fight," he said. Then his hand gripped tighter around mine. "But afterwards, I feel *weak*."

I gave his hand a little squeeze back and looked down into my lap. I didn't want him to see the tears starting to well up in my eyes. My heart was breaking for him. He had to take a shot that made him feel weaker to keep his condition from getting worse. A helpless fury rose in my chest. This wasn't fair. None of this was fair.

"It's kinda one of the side effects," he added after some time.

His gray eyes were big and soft, and I wanted to say so many things to him, but I didn't know how to say it, so I just held his hand and leaned my head on his shoulder.

"I wanted to show you," he mumbled, his voice low. "See if . . . I dunno. I guess to see if you wanted to help."

"Of course," I answered quickly. "Of course I'll help you. Just teach me how." I hoped he couldn't hear the shakiness in my voice.

A sad smile broke across his face, and his eyes crinkled. I wanted to hug him and tell him that he wouldn't have to deal with this alone again, but my throat was too choked up with nerves.

"I'll fill up the syringe myself, then I'll need your help," he said.

I gave him an encouraging nod and Hunter uncapped the syringe and stuck it into the rubber seal on top of the vial, drawing out the liquid.

He flipped the tip of the needle up and tapped the syringe lightly, before squirting a little bit of the amber fluid out of the top. I watched his actions closely. If Hunter and I were going to have a future together, how many times would I have to help him with his injection? Twenty? A hundred? I had to pay attention. He was showing me the reality of his life and I couldn't mess this up. The gravity of the situation was heavy and suffocating, but I knew I had to do this.

"Can you open up one of those alcohol pads?" he asked, pointing to the the shiny foil packets .

I pulled out one of the packets and tried to rip it open. The packaging seemed to be designed to be difficult. Even after I twisted the damn square every which way it wouldn't tear. The harder I tried, the more slippery it got in my clammy hands. Every failed attempt was making my hands shake harder.

"Damnit," I threw it on the bed, frustrated.

Hunter watched me but didn't make a comment, he just reached into the black bag to give me a new foil packet.

I sucked in air through my teeth, then wiped my sweaty hands on my jeans before taking the shiny square from him. I wasn't going to give up. This time, it tore open with ease.

The sharp smell of rubbing alcohol greeted my nose. Hunter unbuckled his belt with one hand and slid his pants halfway to his knees. An image of Aunt Caroline walking in on us flashed through my mind before I burned it out with a vengeance. I had to focus on Hunter right now.

"Just rub the pad on my left thigh," he said, pointing to an area on his leg. "Right here is fine."

I swabbed his skin at the spot he was pointing to, the alcohol evaporating quickly from my fingers and making them cold.

"Here," he said after I threw the pad out. He held the syringe between two fingers and offered it to to me.

I paused to take several deep breaths before accepting it from him. The syringe felt heavier than it looked, like it was made of stone. Sweat beaded on my brow, making my head itchy and uncomfortable. I tried to hold the needle upright, but my hand was shaking furiously.

"Lorrie, can you do this?"

"I don't want to mess up," I croaked. "I don't want to hurt you."

He gave my shoulder a light squeeze. "You won't. I trust you."

I looked into his soft gray eyes, blinking away the stinging in my own. This wasn't about me, this was about Hunter. He was showing me that he could trust me with his pain. If I didn't do this, it would hurt him more than anything else I could possibly do. I had to be brave. I couldn't let him down.

"Inject it right where you swabbed me. It needs to hit the muscle, then you just push the plunger in."

I nodded, swallowing a few times but unable to get rid of the tightness in my throat. My heart raced.

I can do this.

It felt like I couldn't breathe. I was near the edge of panic, but I wasn't going to let emotions get to better of me.

Hunter trusts me.

Closing my eyes I forced myself to take a large lungful of air.

I can be strong for him.

In one quick movement, I stuck the needle into his thigh and pressed my thumb down on the plunger, pushing the liquid into him.

We both let out a sigh.

We had done it. Together.

After my hand stopped feeling shaky, I plucked the syringe out and handed it to him. He capped the tip of the needle and put it back into the pouch. A small droplet of blood dotted the point where the needle went into his thigh and Hunter smeared it away with his thumb.

I took deep shuddering breaths, feeling a numb tingling in my fingers.

Hunter put his pants back on, and then sat down on the bed again. He reached a hand to the back of my neck, pulling my face in until our foreheads were together.

"Thank you," he said, eyes closed and breathing slowly.

"Thanks for letting me help," I whispered back.

Hunter looked directly at me, an intense expression on his face. We held each other for a few moments, taking deep breaths and trying to gather ourselves again.

It felt like we had passed another milestone today. I knew that Hunter didn't really need me to help with his injection. He could have easily done it himself. What he'd done was *choose* to let me see the pain he was dealing with.

Everyone saw the tattoos and muscles, but Hunter had shown me something deeper today. He wasn't a mountain of meat that could take any abuse thrown at him in a cage. He was real. He had hopes and dreams and a heart bigger than that of anyone I'd ever met. I had broken that heart once, but he still came to find me.

Now, he wasn't hiding his problems from me anymore and we were finally starting to face them together. It was terrifying, but I knew that I was at least strong enough to not run away. The mess we had made of things while we were at Studsen seemed like it was so long ago.

I studied his face closely. Many of the bruises he had from the fight were already starting the turn yellow.

"How are your injuries feeling?" I asked.

"They're healing. I think I'll be fine."

I threw my arms around Hunter and pecked him quickly on the lips. His eyes brightened and shot up, a slow smile spreading across his face.

"What was that for?"

"I don't know, just because," I said, smiling back.

He gave me a hug and I sank into him, putting my head on his chest. I could hear his heart beating right next to my ear. I briefly thought about telling him about the letter that I had written back to Marco, but then decided against it. I didn't want to ruin this moment with talk about my mother's murderer.

Hunter and I just held each other, basking in the moment. I wanted this to last forever.

"How long can you stay?" I asked. "You can't just skip all your classes."

He paused a moment before answering. "Well, thing is . . . after I got knocked out at that fight, I applied for a leave of absence. Arrowhart was cool about it, since they know about my MS and all."

My mind raced, processing the fact that Hunter had dropped the semester. He hadn't dropped out entirely, but still, this was a big deal.

"But I thought you were so close to graduating," I said.

"I couldn't focus on school with you gone and I needed some time to recover anyway. Don't worry about me graduating, I only have a few credits left. I can probably just take them online when I need to."

I frowned but didn't say anything. Hunter had been doing pretty well in school, or at least a lot better than me. If he thought he had it under control, then it was probably fine.

"What are you planning on doing in the meantime?"

"I just want to stay close to you right now. At some point, I was thinking of moving to a motel or something, I don't want to impose on your aunt and uncle. I've got some money left over from my fights so it's cool."

My heart danced with joy. I gave Hunter a big wet kiss on the lips. We still had a lot of things to deal with but at least we'd have some time to figure them out.

Chapter Nine
FUN AND GAMES

Hunter had told me he was usually weak after his treatment, but the next day he seemed pretty normal. A little tired, maybe, but nowhere near as bad as I feared.

The whole family spent most of the day lounging around the house. The only exception was when I went with my uncle to get a new phone. Hunter stayed behind to rest.

When we got back, he seemed animated and generally much more like himself, so much so that he volunteered to help with dishes after dinner.

"How are you feeling?" I asked, once my aunt and uncle were out of earshot. The boys had already left to go play.

"Good," he answered.

I waited for more, but he didn't offer anything else. Shrugging, I turned to get another dish from the counter and found one of the kittens on the counter, pawing at the food on a plate.

I cried out in surprise and Hunter snapped his head around. "Bones!" he said sternly. "Get down!"

Bones froze for a second, then scurried away. Shaking my head, I went back to the dishes.

After a little while, I noticed Hunter watching me. "Is something wrong?" I asked, turning to him.

He stuck his lower lip out and shook his head. "Nope. Was just looking to see if I think you might wanna go out tonight. I'm starting to think you're getting a little stir-crazy."

I bit my lip and thought about it. He was kind of right. The trip with my uncle to the mall had been the only time I'd been out other than therapy since I'd come back from Studsen.

Still, though, how would my aunt and uncle feel about us going out? They said they wanted whatever was best for my happiness, but I didn't want to disrespect them.

"We could go out," I said tentatively. "But I don't think we should go anywhere that involves drinking. Beyond the problems with driving drunk, I don't think my aunt and uncle would like it."

"No problem," Hunter said. "I have something in mind I think you'll like."

I thought about asking him if he was sure he was up for it, but stopped myself. That would make him feel like I was treating him as a patient. He could be responsible for his own limits.

"Okay," I said. "Where is it?"

He smiled. "It's a surprise."

I pursed my lips, but the look on his face brought a grin to my face. "Sounds good."

We finished up the dishes, told my aunt and uncle we were going out—they asked us not to be out too late—and soon we were in Hunter's car, on the way to his surprise destination.

A smile played on my lips as we got close. I knew my way around Eltingville well enough to know where we were headed.

Hunter noticed my expression. "Have you guessed where we're going?"

"You're taking me to the carnival!" I said happily.

He laughed. "I guess it was ambitious to try to surprise you in a town you know better than I do."

"No, it's perfect. Thank you for thinking of this."

We pulled into the parking lot a minute later. "You're gonna love this next bit. Close your eyes."

I obeyed, still excited with the prospect of the carnival. Hunter reached noisily behind him to the back seat, retrieved what he had been looking for, and then sat forward again.

"Alright," he said. "Open your eyes."

When I saw what it was, I squealed in delight. He had brought the bag of art supplies I had left at school. A sketchbook and several pens were contained inside. He even brought the portfolio I had been working on for the art competition.

"How did you get these?" I asked.

"Daniela helped me out. I asked her if there was anything important you might've left behind and she gave me this."

I couldn't believe she had managed to keep the secret from me. A stupid grin on my face, I scooped up the bag into my lap.

"Thank you so much!" I said. "This was really thoughtful."

I leaned over and gave him a quick kiss. He smiled and looked generally satisfied with himself. "Glad you're happy with them. You know, you can still mail in your portfolio to enter the competition."

"But I'm not on campus anymore."

"You're on leave right? If you can still submit it, I think you should give it a shot."

Maybe that would be good. Aunt Caroline had suggested that focusing on something would help me recover. This could be just what I needed.

"Yeah. I think I might do that." I smiled at Hunter. He was so encouraging.

"Alright, ready to go? We gotta find you some things to draw."

I nodded happily. We got out of the car and went into the carnival, my art supplies in hand. Unlike when Hunter had taken me to the abandoned amusement park, this carnival was brightly lit and full of life.

The place wasn't overcrowded, but it definitely seemed like the most popular attraction in town. Most of the people there were either high school students or couples like us. The mix of screams, music, and loud conversation made it very noisy.

We walked around the grounds hand in hand, playing a few games and eating sweets. I was on the lookout for something fun to sketch.

A familiar voice came from my right. "I hope you are recovering well."

I stopped in my tracks and turned, a chill running down my spine. *Marco*.

But he was nowhere to be seen. I sucked in deep breaths and turned back to Hunter, who looked at me worriedly.

"You alright?" he asked.

I didn't want to bring our evening down by talking about Marco. It wasn't a big deal anyway, it was probably just because this was the first time I'd been out of the house in a while. I looked around the area for something to talk about so we could change the subject. When I saw a game that measured the player's strength punching a bag, I had just the ticket.

I motioned to the game with my free hand as we walked near it. "Think you can win top prize on that game?" I asked, trying to keep my voice steady.

Hunter flashed me a suspicious look, but his expression changed when he saw what I was talking about. "Come on. I'll break the game."

"Wow," I said, grateful for my quick thinking. "You sound confident."

"I am," Hunter said with a smirk as we walked over to the tent.

A crowd of high schoolers were gathered around watching the biggest guy in their group take his shot at the game. After some encouragement from his friends, he wound up and took a big, wild swing. The bag shot back with a loud thwack and a digital score appeared on the board.

"Seventy-two hundred!" the operator boomed. "Ya need ten thousand to get Bernie. Wanna try again?"

I looked around the booth to see who "Bernie" was and found the answer in a pile of giant stuffed St. Bernard dogs. They were easily four feet long and super cute. Maybe I never had a pet dog when I was younger, but a stuffed one would make me happy now.

"If you're so confident, then I want one of those dogs," I said, pointing at the prizes.

Hunter looked over at me and flashed a grin. "No problem, babe."

The operator, a balding man with a thin, gray mustache and black wireframe glasses that sat a little too low on his nose, was already scanning for his next customer. He knew before the high schoolers had even left that they weren't going to use any more of their tickets on this game.

"Does the little lady want to try her punching power?" he asked, as the previous group was still meandering away. His voice was scratchy, which made me think he was a smoker.

I looked to Hunter, who spoke up. "I do."

The operator looked at the prizes behind him quickly then gave Hunter a gap-toothed smile. "Alrighty, son. That'll be one ticket."

Hunter handed over the ticket and then quickly removed his sweatshirt. His back and shoulders bulged against the thin white t-shirt he wore underneath. His natural scent washed over me in a quick wave, causing my skin to flush.

The operator's eyebrows shot up when he saw Hunter getting prepared. "Making sure you're unimpeded, I see. Do you work out?"

Hunter smiled in the way he did when people were patronizing him. "Just tell me when to punch the bag."

"Step right up. Whenever you're ready."

Hunter wound up and hit the bag with a ferocious straight right hand. Whereas the previous puncher had taken a wild, looping swing, Hunter's motion was tight and efficient.

The bag smacked hard against the machine with a sound between a car backfiring and a gunshot. Some people walking by stopped in their tracks to see what was going on.

A low whistle emerged from the operator's lips. "Twenty-seven thousand, two-hundred," he said, almost to himself.

Hunter looked satisfied with himself. "Let's have the dog, please."

The operator picked up one of the Bernies and handed it to him, still stunned. "Highest score I ever seen on that thing. That was some nice form. You box?"

Hunter handed me the stuffed dog and turned back to the operator. "Kinda."

The operator nodded. "Well, you should keep it sharp. I dunno if you're from 'round here, but there's a gym in town where you could get some work on. Clint might even give you some work if you wanna train some youngins"

"Gotcha. Maybe I'll check it out. Thanks for the tip."

"My pleasure. Hope you enjoy that dog Little Lady."

"Thanks," I said, giving the dog a big hug.

Hunter smiled and put his arm around me as we walked away, his sweatshirt over his other shoulder. People walking by stared at the giant stuffed dog in my arms. It made me feel like a celebrity.

"When did you start boxing, anyway?" I asked, after we'd been walking for a little while.

Hunter squeezed my shoulder a little bit. "I boxed and wrestled in high school, but I didn't get into MMA in college until after I got kicked out of Air Force ROTC."

Of course. That's why he had an Air Force shirt, and his place was so neat.

"Is ROTC why you studied Physics?"

"Yeah, it's a good major if you wanna get into the Air Force. Shows you're disciplined, and having that kind of knowledge is useful for all sorts of stuff in the military."

"Why dId you get kicked out?"

"It was 'cause of my MS. Air Force policy."

"I'm sorry," I said quietly.

"It was something I'd been working for since I was in high school. I just wanted to get up in a plane and fly away from all the bullshit, but whatever. It's over now." He looked down and kicked a rock out of the way.

It must've been difficult for him, to have his dreams dashed, just because of some disease that he couldn't control.

"It's never a bad thing to chase your dreams," I said. Trying to distract him, I decided to bring up something that had been on my mind lately. "I wish I had some idea of what I want in the future."

He shrugged. "No big deal, you got a lot of time to figure it out."

"I think it might help me move on if I figured it out sooner rather than later."

"What about art?" he asked, pointing to the sketchbook in my arms.

I thought about it for a second. He did have a point. Art was something I was naturally drawn to.

"Yeah, maybe. I'm thinking about it. I don't think I was doing super well at Arrowhart anyway. None of those classes were very interesting. I know Daniela really liked her psych classes, but I never got into any of them."

"Maybe you can go to art school or something."

I nodded, staring into the distance. It seemed scary, but maybe it was something I could look into.

"If I had a ton of money, I'd pay for your drawings," he said, his eyes crinkling with his smile.

I smiled and hugged him close, giving him a kiss on the cheek. I could tell he was still a little bothered about our talk about the Air Force.

We came to the food court and took a seat at a free table. Hunter went to go get some food while I sat my new stuffed animal next to me and got out my drawing supplies. Maybe I could draw him something to try and bring his spirits up.

I looked around to see if there was anything good to sketch, before deciding on what I wanted. Working quickly, I began a sketch of Hunter at the punching game, adding plenty of my own twists.

By the time he came back with our treats, I was already well on the way to finishing up. I hid it with my hand as he approached.

"Whatcha working on?" he asked, putting the plate with a funnel cake in front of me.

"Don't look," I said. "I'm almost done."

He chuckled and looked away. "Alright. Don't let your snack get cold, though."

"I won't."

A minute later, I picked up the sweet pastry—which was still warm—and turned my sketchbook so Hunter could see my handiwork. He took one look at it and laughed.

"Is that me?" he asked.

"Yup. I did take some artistic liberties . . ."

"Is that why I'm wearing a cape with a hammer on it?"

I smiled. "Yeah. I mean, technically, it's a drawing of your alter-ego The Hammer as you rescue Bernie from the clutches of the evil Carnival Man."

He pointed at the depiction of Bernie. "Why is Bernie wearing a cape too?"

"Bernie is your sidekick. He's gonna be there to protect you."

He stared at the drawing for a second longer before looking up. "And where are you?" he asked, locking eyes with me.

His expression sent a warm surge through my body. "Waiting for you in your bed so I can polish your hammer after a hard day of saving the world," I said mischievously.

His mouth opened slightly and he licked his lips, then looked away. "We should probably head back after this, don't you think?"

I took a giant bite of powdery sugar goodness. "Sounds good to me."

Fifteen minutes later we were in Hunter's car driving back home. Bernie was riding in the back seat with my art stuff.

"That was fun," I said, staring out the passenger window. "I love my aunt and uncle, but getting out and away from them for a bit was nice."

"Yeah it was fun. I like your aunt and uncle though. Seeing a functional family is kinda a new experience for me."

"What do you mean?" I asked, before I could think better of it.

"My parents are deadbeats," Hunter said simply. "Best case, they ignored me. Worst case, they wanted to get me involved by beating up their dealer or something. It was kinda a lose-lose."

"I'm sorry I brought it up."

"It's okay," he said as we passed by the Perkins house. "It just makes me wonder if I could ever have a happy family. Like putting myself in your uncle's shoes is hard. I kinda wonder if I could do that because I don't really have any role models for it."

"Well you don't have to worry about that for a while. Speaking of my uncle, you missed their house."

"I know."

He looked at me with a wicked grin and drove for a couple minutes more before pulling over in a secluded area under some trees at the end of a cul de sac.

"What are you doing?" I asked, an edgy heat rising in my core as I anticipated the answer.

"What do you want to do?" he replied. His eyes on me, he unbuckled his seatbelt and ran his fingers through my hair.

His touch sent a charge through me, and I began to breathe unsteadily. Had it really only been a few weeks?

"Hunter, I . . ."

I trailed off. Hunter pulled his hand away, though he kept his gaze on mine. "If you don't want to or you aren't ready, I understand. I just thought—"

I grabbed the hand he'd pulled away and brought it back. "Do you have a condom?" I whispered, my heart beating in my ears.

A smile cracked across his face as he dug into his pocket and held up a gold foil package with black letters.

I bit my lip and turned to get out of the car.

"Where are you going?" he asked.

"Back seat."

I opened the door and stepped out. The doors clicked unlocked, then he got out of the car, turned around and opened the back door.

He looked at me over the car. "Get in," he said.

I opened the back door, got in, and closed it. He followed, and we were together in the back seat, sitting like we were expecting the driver to get in any moment.

With Bernie in the corner. Hunter grabbed the stuffed animal he had won behind its head and shoved him to the front seat. "I don't think Bernie wants to see this."

I laughed. "It kind of smells like kittens back here."

Hunter shrugged, then brought his hand behind my head and kissed me warmly on the lips. The heat of his mouth was a pleasurable contrast to the cool spring evening. Our tongues tangled deliciously. This time there was no holding back.

Gradually, Hunter got onto his knees on the seat and rocked me onto my back, my legs on either side of him. His hand still cradled my head, keeping it from hitting the door. His free hand came around my back and I felt the familiar sensation of his fingers on my bra clasp.

"You're sure this is okay?" he asked. "I don't wanna go too fast."

I grabbed his cock through his jeans, and its responsiveness to my touch caused a shiver of excited energy to pass through me. Every hair on my body stood on end. He was hard and getting harder.

"Yes," I whispered breathlessly.

He unclasped my bra and brought me to sitting up to remove my shirt. The air was cold against my suddenly naked skin.

He seemed to read my mind and removed his sweatshirt and then his undershirt. I felt the warmth of his body heat even before he pressed me close to him. He put his sweatshirt behind me for use as a pillow and eased me back down. The mix of his sweat and natural scent that I had gotten a brief hint of earlier now hung in the air, and it drove me crazy with need for him.

"Hurry up," I urged.

He obliged, rocking back taking off my shoes and socks first, then my jeans and finally my underwear. I pulled the arms of his sweatshirt around my chest to keep warm. Each article of my clothing was deposited into a pile on the driver side of the car. His clothes quickly followed into a similar pile on the passenger side, by my head.

He took off his underwear last. My first glimpse of his cock since he'd come to get me made me wet with desire. I didn't want or need any more foreplay. He needed to be inside me. Now.

"Where's that condom?" I moaned, looking from his thick cock to his face. "I want you inside me."

As I heard him tearing open the wrapper, I closed my eyes and leaned my head back into his hoodie. My skin was flushed and sensitive to every bit of sensation. I hadn't realized until that moment how much I had been waiting for this moment.

The head of his cock pushed against the folds of my sex and paused there briefly, positioning. Then he pushed inside me and I felt myself hug tightly around him.

"Fuck," he groaned, easing his hips into me until I had taken him to the hilt. "You feel so amazing."

"Hunter," I breathed, throwing my arms around his neck and digging my nails in.

He rocked back and then began to ram himself in and out of me, pounding me as if he were putting every bit of energy he could into this one act. Pleasure rippled through me from my core to my fingers and toes. My hands went from around his neck to pawing at his hard chest.

Every second dripped with ecstasy. I felt a body-shattering orgasm slowly building. Hunter managed to find another gear, and his increased urgency told me he was close too.

I cupped his taut ass with both hands as he pumped into me. My entire body clenched in anticipation of my climax.

"Lorrie," he moaned into my ear.

My back arched and came together, my body tightening and then releasing in a rush that made me temporarily unaware of the world around me. Every inch of me soaked in the sensation of my bliss.

Hunter's skin erupted in goosebumps as he came. Even through the condom, I could feel the warmth of his cum. He collapsed against me, spent.

"Wow," I said, running my hand through his hair. We held each other for a few minutes.

Finally, he pulled himself up and then out of me before removing and neatly tying off the end of the condom. He reached to the front of the car and put it in a cup holder. I made a mental note to be sure we threw that away as soon as possible.

He came back and hugged me close to him for a quick post-sex cuddle.

"This is perfect," I sighed. "I don't want you to have to leave."

He touched his fingers to my nape. "I talked to your aunt about that, actually. Or tried to, anyway."

My spine stiffened. "What? When? And when were you planning to tell me about this?"

He furrowed his brows. "Tonight. I'm telling you right now. And I talked to her while you and your uncle were out getting a phone."

"Okay, sorry. What did she say?"

"I said I tried to talk to her. She was having none of it and insisted that she and Uncle Stewart had talked and would be absolutely furious if I moved into a motel. They want me to stay and keep working on the dining room and she wasn't going to discuss the matter anymore."

My eyebrows shot up, and if it was possible my stomach was feeling even more fuzzy than before. "So you're not leaving anytime soon?"

He smiled. "At least not for a while, the dining room is going to take some time. Maybe a few weeks at least."

I hugged him with a big grin on my face. After we felt like we were composed enough, we got dressed and went back to the house. I couldn't be any happier.

Chapter Ten
PERFECT

The next day Hunter and I went on a date to an old movie theater in town and watched a zombie movie from the seventies. It was cheesy enough that the whole theater alternated between laughs and some actual thrills, and we both had a great time.

"Old movie theaters are so much fun," I said as we walked in the front door.

"Yup," he said. "And I didn't even flinch when the zombies came."

I smiled. "I was watching you, babe. Your eyes were closed."

His face fell. "Come on, it was just that one time. I'm getting better!"

I threw my arms around him and gave him a quick kiss on the lips. "It's okay. I still think you're a sexy, brave man, even if you are a wimp when we watch scary movies."

He smiled and went to go hang up his jacket. I pulled my phone out of my jeans pocket and checked it for the first time since we had gone into the movie. I was surprised to see a call from Daniela.

Wondering what was up, I went to my room to call her back. I found the missed call on my phone and put the phone to my ear.

She answered after two rings. "Hey!" she said brightly.

"Hi. Sorry I missed your call. What's up?"

"Not too much," she said. "Just, you know, checking in to get the juice about Hunter."

My heart sank. I'd forgotten to call her the previous night.

"Oh, yeah, sorry. I was going to call you," I said. "Things have just been so busy."

"It's okay, just spill. How has it been?"

I gave her a pretty detailed blow-by-blow of the last couple days, including thanking her for giving Hunter my art supplies. Still, I didn't tell her anything about Hunter's MS, it wasn't my secret to share. She listened patiently and waited until I was done to talk.

"Well I'm really glad it sounds like you guys are going strong again."

Were we going strong? I guess we were. Things sure had changed quickly. "Yeah. I don't know how it's going to work out long-term but we're trying."

"I'm sure you two will make it if you really want to."

I swallowed and listened to my heart pound in my ears. "I hope so . . ."

There was silence for a minute. Thankfully, Daniela changed the subject. "Well . . . the other reason I was calling was to tell you I'm not going to be able to make it to your aunt's place for spring break. I'm really sorry, but I just can't make it work with the flights now. I'm actually doing an alternative spring break in Haiti now. I promise I'll make it up to you somehow."

My heart skipped a beat. I was sad Daniela wasn't going to come, but of course she had her own life to live. "Oh, that's okay. I know life can get crazy, and this sounds like a great opportunity. It's really great that you're going on an ASB. What are you doing in Haiti?"

"We're building houses in the area that got hit by the earthquake. I think it's the same place Sean Penn has been doing stuff. Maybe we'll meet him."

I knew that tone. "Hang on a second. Who's 'we' in this case?" I asked, a smile creeping on my face. "Is there something you aren't telling me about? Or, you know, someone?"

She answered so quickly I could barely understand her. "His name is Kyle and he's pre-med and he's so smart and *so* gorgeous and I really hope you can meet him! He wants to be a psychiatrist."

I laughed. It felt good that Daniela hadn't changed. "I hope so too. Maybe over the summer. How long have you guys been seeing each other?"

"We hooked up last week but things have been going super well and I already feel like we're in love."

I rolled my eyes, but hoped for the best. "Well, it sounds promising. I'll have to Facebook stalk him when I get a minute."

"Yeah. Anyway, I'm really sorry I can't come. I'll make it up to you somehow, I promise."

"Really, it's okay. I'm glad you're doing this ASB thing. It sounds like it'll be fun."

"Thanks."

I stared at the room's light blue walls and thought about when I was going to see Daniela again. "So if you're not coming for spring break, do you know what you're going to be doing this summer? We really need to find a way to meet up."

"Not yet. Waiting to hear back on some internships but if there aren't any openings I might just stay in Studsen and see if I can pick something up. I'll definitely let you know when I figure things out, and we can find some way to meet up."

"What's Kyle doing?" I asked mischievously.

"I don't know. Maybe we'll talk about it tonight."

I knew this tone too. "You're seeing him tonight? What are you two doing?"

"Hanging out. Here, actually. We're going to watch The Dark Knight Rises."

My face grew hot and I said nothing. That night with Hunter in my dorm room felt like forever ago, even if it had only been a month.

Daniela laughed. "You inspired me. I've . . . got some things in mind for him. Anyway, I have to go. He's coming over in an hour and I still have to get ready."

"Okay," I said, my face still warm. "Have fun tonight, and if I don't talk to you, have fun in Haiti. Be safe."

"Oh, we'll be safe. Kyle might have some doubts tonight, but we'll be safe."

My eyebrows shot up. "Wow. Okay. Well, I hope you don't scare him off."

"Handcuffs and body chocolate, Lorrie! He will never see that movie the same way. See ya!"

I giggled and hung up. To her credit, she was probably right. If I knew Daniela, she was going to make sure Kyle wouldn't forget the night his dark knight rose while he was watching the movie.

It was good to talk to her and hear she was doing well. Even though we were probably never going to live together again, she was still my closest girlfriend. I needed to make a better effort to maintain that friendship. Having friends like her made me feel more connected to the real world and not get so trapped in my head.

Still smiling, I walked back to the living room where the family was gathered. Hunter was seated on one couch, while my aunt and uncle were on the other. The boys were on the carpet playing with the kittens, as usual.

"Where did you go?" Hunter asked. "And what are you smiling about?"

I did my best to wipe the smile off my face as both my cousins turned to look at me. "Oh, nothing. Just Daniela up to her usual."

"How's she doing?"

I sat down on the couch next to him. "Good. She's going to Haiti on an Alternative Spring Break to build houses for earthquake victims."

"That's commendable," my uncle said.

"Yeah," I said, laughing softly. "I think she's really going because there's a guy she started seeing who's going."

"Ah," he said.

"Well that's still nice," my aunt said diplomatically.

"Dad, where's Haiti?" Joel asked.

"Next to the Dominican Republic," my uncle answered.

"Where's that?"

My uncle smirked. He enjoyed these little teaching moments with his sons. "They're both on the same island. Kind of close to Florida, I guess."

That was the magic word. "Florida! Dad, when are we going to Disney World again?"

"Yeah!" his brother joined in. "When are we going to Disney World? I wanna ride on the big kid rides!"

Hunter and I laughed as the boys upped the pressure to go Disney World. The night passed in much the same vein. It was amazing how much better I felt than I had a week before. I didn't know what the future held, but for now, everything was perfect.

Chapter Eleven
SECRETS

The next morning we ate breakfast together. After, I did some drawing while Hunter worked on the dining room. It felt good to be doing something positive after I had been barely able to get out of bed the previous week. Waking up then had been agony. Now, I was looking forward to what I was going to do with my day.

Before I knew it, the sound of little feet scurrying through the house came from downstairs, followed by my aunt calling for the boys to stop running. I looked at the clock. It was already three-fifteen. The kids had just gotten home from school.

I put some last touches on a sketch I'd been doing of a real life Bernie working as a ski-rescue dog and headed downstairs to the living room. When I got there, I found the boys already horsing around with Hunter as he "taught them some wrestling moves" while a couple of the kittens alternately watched and scurried out of the way. Aunt Caroline was slicing apples in the kitchen for an afterschool snack.

"Don't be too rough with him, you two," I said with a smirk. They could combine all their muscle any way they wanted, there was no way they were moving Hunter an inch.

That didn't stop it from being fun to try, though. Hunter was on all fours, with Joel on his back and Billy trying to take out one of his arms. The boys squealed with delight when Hunter stood up, Joel still on Hunter's back with his arms around his neck and Billy being lifted off the ground as he clung to Hunter's bicep.

"Megatron!" Billy yelled.

I wasn't sure if Billy thought Hunter was Megatron or he was Megatron. Deciding Hunter had things under control either way, I went to the kitchen to see if I could help Aunt Caroline with the boys' snacks. She had her nose in the pantry when I walked in.

"Hi Aunt Caroline," I said cheerfully.

She poked her head over her shoulder. "Oh, hello dear. I didn't hear you come in the kitchen. Have a good day? You hardly came down from your room."

"Yeah, I got a lot of drawing done. Can I help you with the snacks?"

She straightened her back and turned to me. "That would be lovely," she said. "I don't know why, but I can't seem to find the peanut butter. If you could find it and get some into a dish for the boys' apple slices, that would be super. I'm going to go put in a load of laundry."

She went to the laundry room and I resumed the search for the peanut butter. It ended up being behind some chicken noodle soup cans in the back of the pantry. I took it out, globbed some peanut butter into a dish with a spoon, and set that in the middle of the plate of apple slices.

Finally, I picked up the plate and brought it into the living room where the boys were still wrestling with Hunter. "Snack time," I said brightly.

The boys scampered over, with Hunter close behind. Everyone took a slice and chowed down.

"I don't remember the last time I had apple slices with peanut butter," Hunter said. "Not sure I've ever had it, to be honest."

"Really?" Joel said. "Our mom makes them for us all the time!"

Hunter shrugged and chewed his snack in silence.

A buzzing came from my back pocket. It took me a while to realize what it was. I was still getting used to having a phone again.

I pulled it out and looked at the screen. It was a Chicago area code—which I knew from growing up there—but I didn't recognize the number. My lips pursed, I hit answer and put the phone to my ear.

"Hello?"

"Is Hunter there?" the voice on the other line asked. It was a woman and she sounded vaguely familiar, but I couldn't quite place it.

"Who is this?" I asked, putting the plate down on a coffee table. Hunter looked at me questioningly as I walked out of the room for some privacy, stopping at the foot of the stairs.

"He's there, isn't he? I knew it."

That tone of voice was familiar. Finally I recognized it. "Is this Ada?"

There was a brief silence on the other line. I was right. "Yeah," she said. "You need to put Hunter on the phone right now."

Her tone was irritating. Who the hell did she think she was to call me and start giving me orders? "How did you get my number? Why are you calling?"

She sighed loudly, then continued in a condescending tone. "Hunter might die if he doesn't get a test he skipped out on."

My stomach dropped and I felt my pulse pounding in my ears. What the fuck? Was she lying? Why would she lie about something like this?

". . . I'm trying to get him to take it. Are you fucking listening? Is he there?"

"What?" I asked, my voice shaky. "A test?"

"At the hospital, yes. I was there with him after he got knocked out. The doctor told him he had to take this test at the end of the week to make sure his MS didn't start to get worse. They said worst-case scenario, he could die. Like maybe in a few months."

"How do you know he didn't take it?"

"Is he there or not?"

I closed my eyes. "Yes, he's here."

"Good, I knew he'd go chasing you after you ditched him again," she said, speaking quickly. The pattern on the wallpaper was starting to look like it was moving, and my breath came in short bursts. "I was worried he would drop everything and go after you. Looks like I was right. I tried texting him but he didn't respond. Classic Hunter, avoiding a test like this. He has multiple sclerosis by the way. I don't know if he's told you yet."

I bit my lip, trying to steady myself. Ada's petty insults weren't worth getting upset over, but how could Hunter have hidden this from me? Why was he skipping out on this test? It sounded like it could be something serious. Despite her obnoxious tone, even Ada wouldn't lie about something like this.

"I also tried calling him and left messages, because, you know, I really wanted to talk to him and was worried that he had just disappeared. Well, that and I'm not an emo, callous bitch."

That was enough. Maybe Ada really did care about Hunter's well-being but I didn't deserve her bullshit. I opened my mouth to say something back, but closed it and took a deep breath to steady myself. Arguing with Ada wasn't worth my breath.

"He did tell me he has MS," I said, my voice steady. "Is there anything else I should ask him about, or will he know what I mean when I ask him about the test?"

"Put him on the phone."

I shook my head even though she wasn't there. "If he wants to talk to you, he has his own phone."

She let out a frustrated sigh. "I need to talk to Hunter. Don't be jealous that I'm the only one who can convince him to stop being a fucking baby."

Ada could insult me all she wanted, but hearing her talk about Hunter like that, when he was the one who had to deal with so much, made me furious.

"I'd reach through this phone and slap you right now, but that would be child abuse. Anything else?"

"Put him on the phone you stupid fucking whore!"

"Thank you for calling," I said sweetly. "Goodbye."

I held the phone away from my face but I could still hear Ada yelling profanities at me over it. Then I hung up.

Chapter Twelve
TALK

I looked at my phone and contemplated what to do next, putting Ada out of my mind. I had to focus Hunter right now. My face felt hot. Why wouldn't he take this test? How could he hide it from me? If Ada hadn't called, I would have never known about it. It was hard to believe. After we'd had that heart to heart, and he'd told me he wouldn't hide anything like that from me again, here we were. Again. The more I thought about it, the angrier I got.

I shook my head and walked back into the living room, feeling Hunter's gaze on me as I came in and sat on the couch. He searched my face, but I did my best to wipe any expression away, burying my frustration.

"Did you guys finish the apple slices?" I asked.

I was looking at Hunter, but it was Billy who answered. "There's still a couple left," he said. Peanut butter clung to the edges of his mouth. "Do you want some?"

I shook my head in answer as my aunt came into the room. "How are my boys doing?" she asked.

"Good," they answered, nearly in unison.

"Billy, come here and let me wipe your mouth."

"Mommm," he cried. But he stomped over obediently.

I looked at Hunter and felt a jolt as we locked eyes, then looked away quickly. Even though I wanted to yell my voice hoarse at him, I knew it wasn't the right thing to do.

Why had Hunter not taken the test? Was it because he was so concerned about my well-being that he couldn't stay in Studsen? No, that didn't seem right. After the first night he came here, he had plenty of time. Even with him working on the dining room for Aunt Caroline, he would have had time to slip out to go to a clinic in Indiana if he had wanted to.

No, it had to be something else. I sat on the couch, my emotions in turmoil as I tried to figure it out.

It was only when I thought back to the night he let me help him with his treatment shot that I realized what it was. My heart clutched in pain at the realization.

He must be scared.

It was hard for me to imagine how scary it was to deal with something like MS, but I knew it must've been terrifying. I knew that sometimes things were so hard to deal with you didn't deal with them well.

Avoiding the test was not the right thing to do, but I knew what it felt like to be so paralyzed that you couldn't even think straight. I also knew that Ada's approach of yelling at him would never work. The fact Hunter wouldn't respond to Ada's messages was evidence of that.

I took a deep breath and chanced a look at him again. His head turned simultaneously, and his raised eyebrows showed he was concerned by the conversation I'd just had.

"Do you want to go for a walk?" I asked him. The boys—Joel from his position on the floor and Billy still being attended to by his mother—snapped their heads over toward me with enthusiastic looks.

"Yeah, let's go for a walk!" Joel cried.

I grimaced and looked at my aunt, who had already seemed to catch my drift. "We can go for a walk later," she said. "Let's go and clean our rooms first."

Their faces fell. "But Mom! We just cleaned them!"

"Then we can tidy up. Come on, let's go and leave Hunter and Lorrie alone."

They left, the boys grumbling the whole way up the stairs. When the living room was empty, I asked again. "So, do you want to go for a walk?"

Still looking at me carefully, he shrugged and grabbed his black hoodie from the floor. "Sure."

I stood up and went to the closet to get my coat. He followed close behind. We said nothing else before walking out the front door. My stomach quivered nervously as I contemplated the conversation we were about to have.

I broke the silence once we were outside. "Want to go out back to the spot we talked last time?"

"Talk?" Hunter asked, his jaw tense. "I thought we were just walking?"

I cringed. "We can do both."

He looked down at the ground and said nothing. My chest tight, I led the way nervously around the house and toward the path through the woods.

After a moment of walking on the woodchip covered path, I couldn't take it anymore. I pressed my lips together and tried to steady myself, then said the words I'd been rehearsing in my head.

"Hunter, I really care about you, and I appreciate how you've been working on building a healthy relationship together with me. It means a lot."

He thrust his hands into his the pockets of his hoodie and waited a beat to make sure I was finished. "I really care about you too," he said.

He kicked the wet ground and sent a stone skidding along the dirt. "Who called?"

I took one more deep, anxious breath. "Ada."

His eyes opened wide and his mouth opened then shut quickly. It was hard to tell if he was mad, shocked, or both. "Why does she have your number?"

I said nothing, but my vision blurred with unexpected tears. Not wanting him to see them, I turned my face away.

"And what the *fuck* is she doing trying to mess with us? What did she say, anyway? Was she a bitch?"

After wiping my eyes, I steadied myself and looked at him, my heart in my throat. "Hunter, you know what she said."

"She's always been jealous, ever since she and I broke up."

"Why did you skip out on the test?" I asked. My hands were shaking.

He stopped walking. His eyes moved furtively back and forth like a caged animal as he looked at me nervously. Finally, he seemed ready to snap. He turned and whipped his leg viciously to kick a tree along the side of the forest path with his boot. Then he wound up and punched the tree's trunk, sending a large chunk of bark flying.

"FUCK!" he growled, the sound coming from the back of his throat.

His outburst wasn't loud, but it carried the intensity of a gunshot. Tears flooded my eyes and adrenaline surged through my veins. I backed away. "Hunter stop," I choked out. "You're scaring me."

He turned to me, fists in a ball with his right hand bleeding. His eyes looked out of focus for a moment, then his expression melted and his shoulders slumped, defeated. "I'm sorry," he said, breathing hard. "You know you don't have to be scared of me. I'd never hurt you."

He took a step toward me, then seemed to think better of it and stayed put, his eyes on the ground. We stood in the path, still fifty yards from where I had intended to have this conversation. Some robins sang and filled the painful silence. My heart pounded in my ears as I waited for his answer.

When he looked at me, I thought his eyes might be glistening, but I wasn't sure. "If someone could tell you the exact day you were gonna to die, would you want to know?"

Shards of pain splintered in my chest.

"I mean from natural causes," he added. "Like, if they could tell you when your body is gonna just stop working. Would you rather know, or find out when it happens?"

My breath caught in my throat as I thought about "natural causes." My stomach felt like a rock.

He seemed to be waiting for my answer, but when he saw that I had none, he continued. "I can tell you what I think. I wouldn't wanna know. Actually, I don't wanna know, 'cause I don't have to pretend whether this is a real question. I'm pretty sure even though I have MS, I can still make that decision."

The hair on the back of my neck was on end. I ran through his question again and again nervously in my mind. "Of course this is your decision," I said unsteadily, though I looked him in the eye, "I just wish we could have talked about it."

"What is there to talk about?"

"I mean, you haven't even taken the test yet. Maybe it won't be as bad as you think."

He scoffed. "What? Like they'll scan me and then suddenly I'll be magically cured? I know better than that."

"No, but you can't just imagine the worst case scenario either. You have to stay positive."

A sick smile crept over his lips, like he had his own personal joke about what I'd said. "Okay. Hey, I'm positive!" The smile left, and the look that replaced it was painfully earnest.

"Why are you mocking me?" I asked, feeling slightly hurt. "Positivity *is* really important for dealing with this kind of thing."

"I'm sorry. I just don't see the point of getting the test done if there's only going to be bad news."

"There must be a reason the doctors wanted you to do it. Is it possible that they can treat you better if they knew what was going on?"

He paused for a second, and then looked down to the ground, kicking a rock out of his way. "I—I don't know. Maybe."

"If they can, then I think you should give them a chance to help you."

He took a couple deep breaths. It looked like he was trying hard to hold himself together.

Tears flowed freely down my cheeks. Watching him struggle with this broke my heart. "You know I'm committed to us whatever you decide. I'm just hoping you'll let me help when you have to face this stuff."

"And if—if things get bad? Will you still be there?"

"Of course. Of course I'll still be there. I—" I swallowed, my mouth thick. "I'm terrified and I'm still trying to adjust to it, but I'll be there for you."

He shook his head and ran his hands through his hair. "Even if it gets really bad? Even if you have to deal with another early death?"

His words stabbed me to the core. He had always been there for me, I could hardly even think about what

I would do without him by my side without sobbing, but I looked away for a moment and tried to keep it together.

"I'd cry," I said, turning back to look him right in the face. "I'd be devastated. But I'm not running away anymore. No matter what happens, we can face it together. No matter what. I promise. "

Hunter looked away, staring intently at nothing in particular. I knew he was considering my words so I didn't interrupt him, I just let him think. However it made me feel, he had to make the decision for himself. I could be there for him, but this was about him, not me, I knew I couldn't make this choice for him.

Finally, he let out a long shuddering sigh.

He turned back to me, and walked toward me for an embrace. I hesitated for a moment, then brought my own arms wide and wrapped them around him, burying my face in his strong chest and letting out a single sob. He held me, his hands on my back, and we just stood there.

He took a deep breath. "I'm gonna call and make an appointment for that scan. Will you go with me?"

I nodded, inadvertently wiping my tears on his sweatshirt. My face felt raw from all the crying in the brisk weather. "Of course."

I pulled back and craned my neck up to kiss him. He seemed to have the same idea, and brought his lips down on mine. Finally we simply held each other and listened to the world around us. Everything was still. Everything continued on.

Chapter Thirteen
A DIFFERENT KIND OF READING

Hunter's appointment was scheduled for one p.m. that Friday. Thursday passed in a blur of anxious anticipation and awkward attempts to pretend everything was fine. And then it was Friday.

The entire day my stomach fluttered so much I thought it wanted to permanently leave my body. Hunter hadn't eaten anything that day because of his scan but I wasn't eating out of sheer nerves.

We decided to volunteer to get groceries so we wouldn't have to tell my aunt and uncle about Hunter's condition. We were standing in the kitchen shortly after the kids had gone off to school, and Hunter took the lead on convincing my aunt. It didn't take much.

"Oh, that's very sweet of you Hunter," she said. "If you're sure, I can give you the list in just a minute."

"Thanks for letting me help out," he replied, a big smile on his face. I stood mute beside him and tried to emulate his expression.

"No, thank *you*," she said. She left to go get her purse, which contained the list. I exhaled as she left. Every day until we got the results was going to be nerve-wracking.

An hour later we were on the road. Hunter had made an appointment at an imaging center near town, about thirty-five minutes from where my aunt and uncle lived. The scan results were going to be read by a specialist on the other side of town who we were going to see the next week.

I watched his hands as he drove and saw he was clutching the steering wheel white-knuckled. Even if he was trying not to show it, he was nervous. We drove in silence for ten minutes before I tried to break the ice.

"You were perfect with my aunt," I said, cracking my best fake smile.

He shrugged. "She's really nice to me."

"I think she can see you put in an effort with her and she's trying to return the favor."

"I guess that's true. Do you know where we're going?"

I looked at my phone, which had the directions to the center. "Yeah, you still have another couple miles before we have to turn."

He nodded, and we drove without conversation for the rest of the trip. I couldn't come up with anything to say that didn't feel awkward, so I said nothing.

Soon we were walking into the imaging center. The waiting room was maybe a quarter full with a lot of worried looking people sitting nervously. It had white walls with health posters plastered periodically and black chairs.

Hunter signed in and we sat down, chatting idly and looking at the old magazines on a nearby coffee table. His name was called and he followed the technician back to the MRI machine.

I took a deep breath and played on my phone while I waited for him to be done. He had said it took twenty to thirty minutes to do the test, so I had a while. I wracked my brain for things I could do for him between taking the test and getting the results, but still nothing came.

Before I knew it, he was back. "Ready to go?" he asked. The tension that had been in his body before seemed to have disappeared.

I narrowed my eyes and then caught myself and opened them wide. If he was relaxed, that was a good thing. "Yeah, of course. Let's go."

We got into the car and headed for town to buy groceries.

"So how was it?" I asked, once we'd been gotten to the main road.

He shrugged. "Fine. The test itself is really no big deal. You just lie still in a machine for a while."

"Did the technician tell you anything?"

"Nah. Just asked if I'd done it before. I said yeah and that was about it."

I nodded and we were silent again. His attitude was making me worried. It was true that the really scary part was going to come when we got the results, but it seemed to me like he was pretending the whole thing didn't even exist.

There wasn't much I could do, though. I didn't want to stress him out if it seemed like he was handling it. After a moment, I turned on the radio and found the local pop music station. We sat and listened to the music without saying much.

Soon we came to the town center of Eltingville. It only consisted of a few square blocks, but there were some clothing stores and coffee shops scattered along the sidewalks, along with a few bars, restaurants, and a small town square where there were free concerts in the summer. None of the buildings were more than a couple stories, but it was a nice little town.

As we drove through the downtown area to get to the other side where the grocery store was, I pulled my aunt's grocery list out of my purse and shut off the radio.

"Wow, you really need to buy a lot of groceries to feed a family," I said, looking down the list.

"Yeah," Hunter said absently. He seemed to have his eye on something and began slowing down.

I looked around. "The grocery store is another couple blocks."

But he was already pulling over and getting ready to parallel park. "I know," he said as he put the car in reverse.

I looked around, confused at why he was parking. 'You know they have a lot," I said, imagining the two of us lugging groceries a couple blocks back to the car.

He pulled forward to adjust and said nothing. It had been a very smooth parking job. "Come on, let's go."

He opened his car door. I stayed put. "Go where? I told you, they have a lot. Why are we parked here?"

"I wanna get our fortunes told."

He motioned with his chin and my eyes followed. Sure enough, a fresh, crisp paper sign was hung in a window on the second floor of the building advertising fortune telling and massage services. Just above that was a sign that said OPEN.

Skeptical, I opened the door and stepped onto the sidewalk. Did he really want to get his fortune told? Now? It seemed kind of morbid, considering the possibilities from the test he had just taken.

"Are you sure?" I asked.

"Of course I'm sure. I pulled over and parked, didn't I? Why wouldn't I be sure?"

I paused a second in panic and then shrugged, hoping he couldn't read my mind. "It's kind of a weird mix, isn't it? Massages and fortune telling?"

"I'll just tell them I want my fortune told and that's it."

"Okay, whatever."

He walked around the front of the car, then held the door to the building for me. I walked inside and he followed closely after.

The smell of incense assaulted our nostrils before we were halfway up the stairs. By the time we got to the fortune teller's suite, I was already feeling light-headed.

The glass door to the suite was locked, but there was a sign telling visitors to hit the button to the right of the door to be let in.

"You sure you want to do this?" I asked, my finger hovering over the button.

Hunter nodded from his place on the top step. "Yeah, I'm sure. Now let's get some fuckin' fortunes read!"

He laughed. I shook my head, uncertain what to think about Hunter's sudden enthusiasm for fortune telling. When I pressed the button, a high-pitched bell sounded from inside.

A woman came to the door. Whatever I'd been expecting, it wasn't this.

She was maybe thirty years old, if that, with long, wavy brown hair and pale skin. Her black drawstring pants were loose-fitting and paired with a white tanktop and a green zip-up hoodie. I was surprised to see she wasn't wearing any shoes. She didn't wear any makeup either, though her natural face was still pretty.

In general she reminded me of the "hippie chicks" at Arrowhart.

She opened the door. "Come in," she said, her voice a high squeak. A fresh, pungent wave of incense and scented candles greeted Hunter and I as we trotted in.

I leaned next to him as our fortune teller was closing the door. "I think all these smells are going to make me high," I whispered.

He shrugged. "Don't think you'll be alone. I'm pretty sure I spell pot."

I giggled and we looked around. A candle burned on every available surface. Across from us, a collection of well-loved books stocked a shelf leaned against the wall. I didn't recognize any of the titles. In fact, I wasn't even sure all of them were in English.

The wall was littered with posters containing strange symbols and seemingly symbolic drawings in pen and ink. I recognized one of them as a particularly complicated celtic knot, but that was it. This definitely didn't feel like Eltingville.

Hunter seemed to be similarly transfixed. I turned to him to make a comment, but he was too engrossed with our surroundings to get his attention.

I heard the door close and the fortune teller scurry behind us. "Can I get you guys anything? Tea?"

We shook our heads. To our right was an old, oak circular table with four cushioned chairs around it. The fortune teller came around it to stand in front of us, putting her hand on Hunter's arm for balance as she did so. I raised an eyebrow but didn't say anything. Instead I looked at her eyes. Hunter was right, they were totally bloodshot. The girl was stoned.

"Awesome. Hi guys, I'm Trinity. What can I do for you today? Massage?"

My head snapped over to Hunter, who opened and closed his mouth once before answering. Part of me just wanted to get out of here. Trinity wasn't exactly filling me with confidence. "We were hoping to have our fortunes read," he said uncertainly.

She nodded and looked to me, a big smile on her face. I kept my expression blank and deferred to Hunter.

"Okay," she said. "Great. Have either of you had a reading before?"

I shook my head and she turned to Hunter. He did likewise.

"Cool. I'm sure you'll enjoy the experience. How about a tarot reading? Is that good?"

I vaguely knew what tarot was, but Hunter was running this show so I again deferred to him.

His eyes narrowed. "Is that the thing with the cards?"

Trinity nodded helpfully.

"Yeah," he said with a shrug. "That sounds great."

She smiled and quoted us her price, which was charged in half-hour increments. Hunter seemed satisfied, and told me he was paying.

The three of us sat down and got situated, with Hunter and I at one end of the table and Trinity on the other.

"So how long have you been doing this?" I asked, still dubious at her age and demeanor.

Trinity shuffled the deck of cards. "Like since I was born. My aunt did fortune telling here for a long time. She taught me growing up. I added the massage thing since I went to school for that and I've been here for a couple years."

"Wow," Hunter said. "So you've been doing this a long time."

Trinity laughed and gave him a beaming smile. "I mean I'm only thirty-one, so it's not that long!"

Wait, was she flirting with him? She cut the cards into three piles. "So who am I doing a reading for?"

Her eyes were still fixed on Hunter, who shifted in his chair. "Can you do one for both of us?"

She shrugged. "I mean we can do whatever you want."

I flashed Hunter a scowl. She was definitely flirting with him, but he was too fixated on Trinity's shuffling.

"Typically it's better to do one person at a time though," she said.

He seemed to be considering this when I stepped in. "Hunter, why don't you get one first since you really wanted to do this? If you want I can get one after."

He bit his lip for a moment but then nodded. "Yeah, let's do that."

Trinity cocked her head to one side and smiled, "Awesome," she said, putting the deck back into one pile. "Let's do this."

She dealt the cards into groups of two, three, and two. When she was done, she put the deck down and studied the cards in silence.

Trying to get Trinity's flirting with Hunter out of my mind, I joined him in studying the cards. Or at least I looked at them. I had never seen cards like this in my life. Some of them had numbers and some of them didn't. There was one upside down in the left group of two and one upside down in the group of three. That was about all I could tell. I sat back and waited for Trinity to tell us what these things supposedly meant. When I looked at Hunter, he was doing the same.

"Mmhmm," she murmured, breaking the silence. "Fire, air, and a drop of water."

Hunter blinked. "What? What does that mean?"

I felt the same. What was she talking about?

She shook her head slightly and pointed to the pair of cards on our left. "This is your past." She moved her finger to the middle. "This is your present." Finally, she pointed to the other pair. "And this is your future."

Her voice was an octave lower than it had been a moment before. I supposed this was her fortune telling voice. Hunter and I both looked at the cards anew, then back at her. For a moment I felt stupid, but then I figured there was no reason to know this stuff anyway.

Trinity continued. "The cards tell me something that began recently has you feeling trapped and burdened."

That could mean anything, but maybe it could be applicable. Confused, I looked up from the cards and found Trinity staring at me intently. More specifically, my boobs.

She looked up and made eye contact, holding it for a second and smiling before I looked away. I turned to Hunter to see if he had just witnessed what happened, but he was too engrossed in his cards.

I looked at him as she moved to the three cards in the middle signifying his present. His expression showed legitimate interest. Why was he suddenly so into fortune telling? And how could be unaware of what was going on with Trinity?

"We're missing air here," Trinity mused, as if she hadn't just been staring at me. "And a messenger has come."

She pointed to a card depicting a knight with a golden cup. Hunter pursed his lips and looked at me. "Are you a messenger?" he asked skeptically.

I shrugged as they both fixed their gaze on me. "I have no idea. I guess maybe?"

"It's basically a message of judgment," Trinity said, pointing to another card.

My brows shot up along with Hunter's. This was getting more bewildering by the minute. "I have no idea."

She pointed to the other card in the group of three and pursed her lips, then gave Hunter a small smile. "Things are about to change, I think. Let's see what your result will be."

I stared at the card she had been pointing to. It was a picture of a guy dancing with a coin in either hand and a really big hat. How that meant change, I didn't know.

Shaking my head again, I watched her study the pair of cards for Hunter's future. She didn't point to anything this time. Instead, she looked Hunter in the eye. "You will find abundance in the darkness."

Hunter nodded and looked at me, then back at her. His expression was one of bemusement. "Can you, uh, explain that?"

She shook her head, her expression somber. "It's what the cards say."

"But that doesn't make any sense! Am I going to like, stumble into some treasure while I'm lost in the woods or something?"

She shrugged, a smile threatening to creep over her face. "Maybe."

His palms were up on the table. "Who the hell finds treasure anymore? Maybe I should go find a time machine and be a pirate? I mean I'm not opposed if you have access to a time machine."

He turned to me. "Lorrie, do you wanna be a pirate?"

It was hard not to giggle at Hunter's outburst. He could be such a goofball. I looked over at Trinity to see if she was offended, but it seemed like she was amused if anything. She raised her eyebrows at me and cocked her head slightly.

I turned away. "It sounds like a pretty positive future to me," I said diplomatically. "And yes, if you want me to be a pirate with you, I think that sounds lovely. Should we get out of here?"

He let out a long breath and then smiled at me. "No way, it's your turn! If you get the pirate fortune too, we're going on a time machine hunt. Or at least buying lotto tickets."

"I don't think we have time," I tried, making a show of looking at the clock and at Trinity.

Hunter wasn't getting my drift. "Come on Lorrie! I'm gonna be a pirate! Life's awesome!"

The grin on his face was so big I would have thought he was drunk if I didn't know better. Was that why he had wanted to come here? Did he just want some laughs?

"I can do a simple three card reading for you," Trinity cooed, bringing the energy of the room back from Hunter's frenzy. "It'll only take a minute."

I sighed and look to Hunter, hoping he would get the message. My attempts to communicate nonverbally were futile. "Do it Lorrie. Three cards!"

"Okay," I said grudgingly. "But I'm blaming you if it's bad."

His face screwed up into a goofy grin and he shrugged. "Deal. I also want credit when it's awesome, though."

Trinity smiled at the two of us and shuffled the deck. She cut it the same as she had before, then dealt the three cards out.

"This reading's easier," she said. "The first card is the past, the second the present, the third the future."

My vision narrowed as I fixated on the third card. It was a picture of a hanged man. A chill jolted up my spine. Hunter seemed to notice it too and looked at me sheepishly.

"Mmm, an all water reading," Trinity said, scanning the cards. "Very interesting."

"What does that mean?" I asked. I was curious despite myself.

Her heavy-lidded eyes pierced through me as she considered how to answer. "You're moving, but things are staying the same."

I nodded slowly, pretending to understand. Hunter had his lips pursed tight.

Trinity's finger moved to my past. "The ace is reversed. Maybe you felt stable but later found you weren't?"

The hair on my neck stood on end as I thought about my family and Marco. An uneasy sensation began to take hold of me. Hunter took a look at me and put his hand on my shoulder.

She seemed to not notice my reaction and moved to the middle card. "It looks like you've been nostalgic lately. Maybe somebody passed away a while ago?"

Her glance moved from the cards to my face. "Aw hey, there's no need to get freaked out. This spread's totally fine."

I shook my head and tried to stop taking this stuff so seriously. It was all coincidence. "But that card is the hanged man," I said, feeling silly even as I uttered the words.

She shrugged. "Yeah, but tarot wise that's more like breaking free most of the time."

"So is someone important in her life going to die?" Hunter asked.

"I mean it could be that too," Trinity said, turning to Hunter. She bit her lip and eyed him suggestively. "But I think we all know which hung man is in her future, am I right?"

Blood rushed to my face.

"We should go," I said, grabbing Hunter's arm.

Trinity's bare foot eased down my inner calf, causing me to scooch back my chair. "You guys sure you don't wanna stay?" she asked, smiling at me. " I do massages too. Even couples."

I stood up, shaking my head. "We're good."

She cocked her head and pouted. "You sure? Why don't you stay anyway? I've got a bottle of vodka in back, and I love company."

I tried to physically pull Hunter out of his chair. This time he got the drift.

"Thanks Trinity," he said, pulling out some cash quickly to pay for our half-hour.

"You guys sure you don't even wanna smoke a bowl?"

The fresh air felt like a return to reality. "Let's never go to a fortune teller again," I said. "That was really weird."

"I dunno," he answered with a laugh. "I thought that was pretty entertaining. Maybe not what I was expecting, but pretty cool."

I slapped him on the arm. "Hunter, she was hitting on us the whole time!"

"Really? I mean at the end yeah—"

"Good lord you're thick."

He pursed his lips, trying to avoid smiling. "That's kinda what she said. . ."

I looked at him, wanting to stay mad, but laughed. It was good to see Hunter in a good mood after his test, even if he had dragged me to a bizarre tarot card reading.

"Why did you want to come here, anyway?"

He shrugged and started walking to the car. "I dunno. Partly trying to loosen up, I guess. I figured with all the worries about my test results, we gotta show ourselves that we're not afraid of the future."

Hunter was right, maybe this was the best way to deal with it. Worrying ourselves to death wasn't helping anyone.

We arrived at the car and got in. "Okay," I said, buckling my seatbelt. "I guess that makes sense."

"Speaking of our futures, I thought our fortunes looked pretty good. I mean, I'm gonna find treasure."

I scoffed. "You didn't get the hanged man card!"

"But she said that was breaking free, right? Or something. Honestly the whole thing was kinda confusing. But treasure!"

"I don't know," I said, putting on my seat belt. "I think I had some brain cells die in there with all the candles and incense."

He shrugged and started up the car. "Alright, so you don't like fortune tellers. Shit's not real anyway. Sorry you didn't have a good time."

I reached over and gave his arm a squeeze. "I'm sorry," I said. "I appreciate the effort to do something fun."

He nodded and, with a lurch from his seriously ancient car, we were off. I spent the rest of the day thinking about how I could keep Hunter's spirits up for the next few days. He was trying hard to stay upbeat, but I was worried that the test was bothering him more than he let on. Still, even if his bravado failed, maybe it was better to face it head on rather than hide from it. Would I be able to face my own issues head on like he had?

Was sending Marco a letter enough of a step in the right direction? I still hadn't told Hunter about it, but I made a note to myself to get his thoughts on it as soon as I had a chance.

Chapter Fourteen
STOLEN MOMENTS

We were in a wood-paneled room with one small window behind the desk. I sat at the front of the wooden desk covered with papers and looked at my interrogator. He was an unfriendly man with a rising hairline trying to act kind and understanding. It didn't suit him.

He leaned forward on his desk. "Alright, just so we're clear: you have no recollection of any events between your mother and Mr. Peralta that would suggest a possible rift growing between the two?"

"That's correct," I said, just as my attorney had taught me to respond. If I said "yes" or "no," that could be taken the wrong way.

"No screaming matches, nothing like that?"

"That's correct."

He put his glasses down and rubbed his eyes for the hundredth time. It was like he was trying to show me his frustration. "No drinking? Drugs?"

"Right."

"Even your mom?" he asked, putting his glasses back on.

I shook my head. "She pretty much quit drinking after she left my dad."

He nodded, then got out of his chair and came around his desk. I scooted my chair back as he took a seat on the desk's edge, his pants uncomfortably close to my face.

"Listen honey, we need a motive, and you're our best shot. You've got to give me something, okay? There had to be some reason this guy killed your mom."

I turned my face away, partly to get away from the prosecutor's crotch in my face, partly to hide my tears. When I turned back, his face had changed.

It was Marco. He reached out for my neck to strangle me. To kill me. Just like he'd killed my mom.

I screamed even as his fingers dug into my neck, cutting off my air. Time passed, his fingers dug further in, and I kept on screaming.

I woke up with a jolt. I had fallen asleep with my laptop next to me, open to the website of an art school. My heart still pounding, I sat up on the couch. This obsession with Marco's motives was getting worse. I hoped I would get a letter back from him soon.

Sitting up, I rubbed my eyes and looked around me. It was already Sunday afternoon and the midafternoon sunlight streamed in through the curtains. The details of the dream were starting to fade away but my heart still beat quickly in my chest. It didn't help my nerves that we would be getting Hunter's test results in only a few days

Aunt Caroline and Uncle Stewart had taken my cousins off to a baseball camp. I had stayed in the living room to browse some art schools while Hunter continued his work in the dining room. Some of the schools looked amazing, but the idea of moving and attending one was pretty daunting. There were a few that weren't even in the United States. After looking at them for too long, I must've dozed off. There was no point in obsessing over that now anyway, we still didn't even know what Hunter's condition was going to be.

The noise coming from Hunter's work in the dining room stopped, and a moment later he was beside the couch. "Hey, let's get outta here," he said. He dried his hands with a paper towel as he talked. "I wanna show you something."

"What is it?" I asked, a little uneasy. The last time he'd wanted to show me something, it had been his MS treatment. Maybe I was just stressed out because we were still waiting on Hunter's test results. The dream hadn't helped my nerves either.

"Don't worry, it's something good. Come on, it's crazy warm out."

He motioned toward the door. It would certainly help me forget about that horrible nightmare and the little smile on his face intrigued me. Plus, it would be a shame to stay in the house all day. Hunter was probably worried about his test results too, and staying in all day while I moped around about my dream wouldn't do anyone any good.

I rubbed my eyes, and yawned. "Just let me get changed real quick, okay?"

He shrugged. "Yeah sure, but hurry up."

"Okay," I said with a laugh. "Where are we going? Since I'm getting dressed."

"You can wear whatever," he replied. Then he seemed to think better of it. "Actually, you probably want shoes you can walk in."

I nodded and walked upstairs. After a few minutes deliberation, I decided on a sundress. Might as well celebrate the first warm day of the year. Thanking myself for shaving my legs in the shower the previous night, I got dressed and bounced downstairs wearing a comfy pair of flats.

Hunter was waiting for me by the door. After making sure I was ready, he led the way to his beat up car out front. He had the directions to where we were going on his phone, but when I asked to be navigator he said no.

"So . . . are you going to tell me where we're going?" I asked once we were on the road.

"It's a surprise," he replied, shooting me a sly grin.

I shrugged and sat back in my seat. The last time he'd surprised me, it had been the carnival. Whatever this was, it was probably good. I felt bad that Hunter had to take charge of cheering himself up, but to this point he had seemed to have his mood under control and I didn't want to make him feel like I pitied him. I knew he hated that.

We rolled down the windows and let the cool spring breeze draft through the car. Hunter drove through the flat roads of Indiana until we were on the freeway. Whatever he had in mind, we definitely weren't going to the fortune teller this time. I was starting to feel better too. The fresh air helped me get my mind off of that nightmare.

"Hey Hunter?"

"Yeah?"

"Thanks for suggesting this."

He laughed. "We haven't even gotten there yet. You have no idea where we're going."

"Yeah, but just leaving the house is helping me relax. I had a really awful nightmare while I was napping on the couch."

"Oh, what about?"

"My stepfather's trial."

"Oh."

I took a deep breath to steady myself. It seemed like so long ago, but talking about it now was still difficult. Even so, I wanted to tell Hunter. I knew it didn't help to keep it inside. "It was kind of a flashback of when they were questioning me about my mom and Marco's relationship. One of the hardest things about what happened was that nobody ever figured out why Marco did it. It's really been bothering me a lot lately."

Hunter nodded, his eyes were on the road, but I could tell from his expression that he was listening.

I continued. "I mean, maybe it would have made sense if he was into drugs or fought a lot with my mom or something, but none of that ever happened. They always seemed happy together. It just never made sense. The prosecutors pushed me and pushed me. They were sure I'd remember something if they kept going through it, but I didn't. I've kept thinking about it even after the trial. Nothing."

"Shit, that sounds really hard."

"Yeah. I think that's what made it so difficult for me to face what happened."

"Do you think you'll ever find out the reason?"

"I don't know, but I wrote him a letter back asking him."

"You did?"

"Yeah. Dr. Schwartz thought it might be good for me, so I did it last week. I don't know if he'll reply, but maybe I can get some answers."

"I hope you can get the answers you want too."

I nodded and turned to look out the window at the trees passing by.

He brought us out here to lighten the mood and here I was talking about depressing things again. I turned back to Hunter and smiled at him, patting his knee. "Anyway, let's not ruin the sunny weather."

Hunter smiled back and put his hand over mine reassuringly.

We sat in silence for a while, each lost in our own thoughts and enjoying the scenery passing by. I couldn't help myself. The wind blowing through my hair made me drowsy and before long I closed my eyes and drifted off. This time, it was a dreamless sleep.

I woke up almost an hour later. As I rubbed the grit out of my eyes, we whizzed by a sign at the side of the road that read "Indiana Dunes National Park."

I had come here once when I was really young, but I didn't remember much. What had caused Hunter to want to take this long trip?

I stretched out, feeling in a playful mood. "Jeez, you drove us a long way."

"Hey Snorrie, you woke up just in time, " he said, a big dopey smile on his face.

"Why the day trip? You know we didn't have to come this far if you just wanted some alone time."

"Well, you've only got a few more days before you gotta submit your portfolio, so I figured you might want some better drawing subjects than the inside of your aunt's place and Bernie."

"Did you—?"

"Yeah," he said, reading my mind. "I got your supplies from your room. They're in the back seat."

I beamed at him. The sun was shining bright and we were already turning onto a dirt road. To either side of the car were vast plains of grass and wildflowers. I watched the scenery go by, getting more excited by the minute. He was right. This would be a perfect place to get some drawing done and really get my mind off my nightmare.

After some more driving, we were pretty far off of the main road and Hunter parked the car in a little patch of gravel.

"This look good?" he asked.

I surveyed the surrounding landscape. We were surrounded as far as the eye could see by rolling dunes and trees. It was perfect.

"Yep," I said. "This is just what I needed. Thank you so much."

We got out of the car. Hunter got a blanket from the back seat and I carried my art supplies. We walked a few minutes until we were away from the car and got set up. Hunter spread the blanket out and plopped down. I unslung my bag of art supplies and did the same.

While he laid down and stared at the sky, I got my sketchbook out and began scanning our surroundings for the perfect subject.

Hunter propped himself up on his elbow and watched me as I made the first tentative lines of a horizon.

"Looks like you're settled," he said. "I'm gonna go look for another spot for you to sketch."

I smiled up at him as he stood up and dusted himself off. "Okay."

With a wave, he turned and headed off. I watched him go for a moment, then went back to my sketch.

Suddenly I had an idea. I looked up and watched Hunter as he scanned the woods looking for a way in. The way he was framed against a particularly large dune in the background under the cloud dotted sky was just perfect.

I tore out the page I was working on and began to quickly sketch the scene before he made it too far. The details could be fleshed out once I had the basics down, but I wanted to capture this moment as best I could.

The basics came together just as he seemed to spot an opening and charged up the hill into a forest of trees. Smiling to myself, I started work on the details.

I'd been working for around forty minutes when he came back into sight. By the time he got back to the blanket, I was just finishing up inking my sketch.

He looked over my shoulder. "Is that me?"

"Yep. I was watching you go when I realized I had the perfect subject."

He grinned. "Well, I found you another one. There's a really cool spot about fifteen minutes walk from here. You game?"

I put my drawing away carefully. "You bet," I said happily.

It took us a few minutes to pack up, then we were off. We walked across the field and then took a turn up into the trees. After winding around a makeshift path through the trees, we came to a hill.

"The spot's just up ahead," he said.

I wanted to ask him how he had found this place but he was already walking up the hill. Hunter got to the top first and flexed his biceps with his chin in the air like he had just won a bodybuilding competition.

I reached him a minute later, a little sweaty.

"Hey, I didn't realize we were raci—" I trailed off when I saw the view, my mouth dropping in awe.

Lake Michigan shimmered bright and blue beyond the small white sand beach. The calm blue waters stretched out farther than the eye could see. Thick green leaves framed the view from the row of trees that lined the hill. Other than the two of us, there was no one else in sight.

A fresh breeze blew my hair across my face, carrying with it the smell of grass and wildflowers, cooling the sweat on my brow.

I turned to Hunter and tiptoed up to kiss him on the cheek. "Wow. This is beautiful. How did you find this place?"

He grinned and spread out the blanket. "Good old-fashioned exploration. Come on, you get to it. I think it's my turn for a nap."

"Okay, let's lay that under a tree, so at least we can lean on something."

Hunter nodded and followed me as we walked along the crest of the hill until we found the perfect spot. He spread the blanket against a nice thick oak tree and sat down at the base. I took a spot next to him, gazing out across the lake.

After I had taken my supplies out of my bag, Hunter rested his head on my shoulder so he could nap. I started sketching the horizon where the lake met the sky but was distracted when Hunter kept nuzzling at my neck.

So much for napping. I ran my fingers through his hair while he left soft kisses on my skin. When I looked at him again his hair was sticking in a few different directions like a bale of hay. There were even some eraser shavings in his hair. I couldn't help but laugh.

"What are you laughing at?"

"You look silly. I don't know if I can keep calling you Gunther Handsome with that hair."

"Hey, you made it that way. Besides, true beauty comes from within."

He nodded sagely.

"Wow," I said, rolling my eyes. "You're so insightful."

"I'll show you insightful."

He leaned in and pressed his lips against mine. I hesitated for a moment, then melted into him, overcome by my desire for the wetness of his mouth. The drawing pad fell to the side, but I didn't care. Even though my aunt and uncle gave us our space, we hadn't had a chance to kiss like this since our night at the carnival.

We finally broke apart, my chest heaving and breathless. Hunter was staring at me intently, a simmering heat in his eyes.

Our lips crashed together again, and a shiver of pleasure ran up my spine. He smelled liked spring and I could already feel the stirring of heat in my core. Hunter's rough hands slid up the loose sundress I was wearing. When his thumb rubbed light circles on my thigh, my insides clenched.

I pulled his face to me, needily. I wanted to taste him right now. I reached towards his body, smiling into the kiss when my hands finally found what they were looking for. Hunter grinned too when I rubbed my fingers lightly up the smooth skin of his tight abs and up to his hard chest. He breathed deeply, his chest moving up and down.

"Look what I brought." Hunter reached into his pocket and pulled out a condom.

I slapped him playfully on the chest. "What made you think you were going to get lucky today? Just because you took me to this great spot?"

"Yeah, I figured once I proved to you how good I am at finding *just the right spot*, there's no way you'd turn me down." He gave me a saucy wink before burying his face into the side of my neck and leaving a fiery kiss there.

My face heated, I checked around us to make sure the coast was still clear. I'd never done this with anyone somewhere so public. There didn't seem to be anybody in sight, but I was still nervous.

"What if someone sees us?" I whispered.

Hunter stopped kissing my neck and looked around, "Well they're gonna have to watch on the sidelines, I know you're not interested in threesomes."

"No! You know what I mean."

"I've been walking around the whole area for the past hour and haven't seen a soul. I'm pretty sure we'll be fine."

I pursed my lips. Maybe I was making too big a deal out of this. He was right. I hadn't seen anyone out and about either.

"Besides, we'll probably hear them coming before they see us anyway."

Chewing on my lip, I ran my fingers down his chest. What the hell? Why not be a little risky today?

He was eyeing me carefully. "So do you want me to find the perfect spot or what?"

I giggled. "Alright, but only if you stop telling those corny jokes."

He mimed zipping his lips shut and tossing away the key.

Then he started leaving a trail of hot kisses down my body through the light fabric of my dress. I gasped at the sudden shift in his mood and my heart pounded in anticipation. His kisses went lower and lower, each one a promise of what he would do to me with his mouth.

Finally, his tongue brushed the inside of my thigh. A small whimper escaped my mouth. Hunter gently spread my legs apart and pulled my panties down around my ankles.

The breeze lifted my dress a little, making me feel exposed and edgy, but it all disappeared when Hunter kissed me between my thighs, teasing my sex. I squirmed as the pleasure rose in waves, and grabbed a handful of his hair, raising my hips up to meet his hot mouth.

He worked long strokes up and down my swollen lips until I was a shuddering mess, before switching to quick circular flicks on my clit. An orgasm built in my core until I was near the edge of madness. He held me there, hovering between tension and release. The hot softness of his tongue pressed against my wetness until I lost track of time.

Then his touch was suddenly gone.

I moaned his name, and became aware of the quiet outside of the distant crashing of the waves. I opened my eyes to see why he he had stopped. Hunter stared at me with a possessive gaze, unbuckling his belt. He ripped open the condom wrapper with his teeth while one hand stroked his cock. In quick efficient movements he sheathed himself while I admired his rigid length. I bit my lip, anticipating the moment that he would enter me.

Hunter rubbed my clit with his cock, teasing me. I pushed myself towards him.

"You're so wet," he whispered, breathless.

I nodded, unable to say anything else, but letting him know with my eyes what I wanted.

Hunter leaned his massive body above me and slid his cock into me, inch by inch. I clutched at his back in helpless pleasure as my sex slicked pussy stretched around his girth.

He moved in and out of me slowly several times. Then he picked up the pace, thrusting himself feverishly into me, as waves of bliss washed over my body. I squeezed his firm hips between my thighs, holding on for the ride, getting closer and closer to release.

I came. My spasms forced me to grind my pussy against him even faster, overloading me with ecstatic sensation.

Hunter grunted, a primal rumbling from low in his chest, as he shuddered and then lay still. The warmth of his semen spilling into the condom inside me turned me on so much, I almost came again.

We held each other, sweaty and breathless. Then he picked off a strand of hair from my face and kissed me. I had never felt so deeply satisfied.

A little while later, when I came back to my senses, I looked quickly around us in a brief moment of panic. But Hunter had been right. We were safe. There was no one was in sight.

He rolled off of me and leaned his head on my chest, still panting lightly. We caught our breaths under the tree for a while, listening to the soft chirping of crickets and the rustling of the water on the beach below.

We didn't say anything else to each other, but we didn't need to.

Chapter Fifteen
STRONG

The next day we dropped by the post office so I could send off my portfolio to the art competition. Hunter even brought a kazoo he borrowed from Joel, which he blew loudly when I dropped the package into the bin. It was silly, but it helped keep our minds off of Hunter's looming test results.

Despite our mini celebration, the rest of the day was tense. We both knew that we would get his results the following day, for better or for worse.

Before we were ready the next day came and it was time to find out the test results. We told Aunt Caroline we were going to the mall and left the house in the afternoon.

Hunter had seemed pretty nonchalant on the drive over, but now that we were at the clinic, he seemed more nervous. One of the lights in the waiting room flickered on and off, buzzing like there was a bug flying around inside of it. I looked at the bright teal colored chair I was sitting in. There were rows of them arranged around the waiting room.

The room was mostly empty except for a middle aged man sitting in a wheelchair and an older lady next to him. They were having a heated whisper conversation. Hunter was at the front desk, giving them his information. When he came back, his lips were a tight thin line. He sat down without a word.

Even though he seemed like he was healthy for the past few days, we both knew that didn't mean anything. He was fighting something that was unseen but very real. Any second it could knock him down without warning.

I could feel the panic starting to rise in my chest but I fought it down with a fury.

"Hey, it's going to be okay," I said. I patted his hand gently.

He looked straight ahead, his jaw clenched. "Yeah. I know."

I didn't know exactly what was running through his head but I could guess. Whatever the results were, I needed to let him know that I would be there for him. I reached an arm around his hunched over shoulders and leaned my head against him. Maybe I could give him some small amount of comfort.

He took shallow breaths, gripping the arms of the chair tightly.

"Do you want some water?" I asked.

"Nah."

I watched his profile carefully. Hunter looked around the room, not volunteering anything else. His sharp gray eyes darted to the man in the wheelchair.

The whispering between the lady and the man on the other side of the room got louder.

"—just why it had to happen to me?" The man had his head in his hands. The lady was patting his back gently, making soothing noises.

Hunter stared at them, his face grim. Maybe it would help if I could distract him.

"Hey," I said as cheerfully as I could. "Do you remember that night when we first met?"

He pulled his eyes away from the conversation across to the room, but he wasn't giving me his full attention. "Hm? You mean at the lake?"

"No, not the lake. I guess that is when we first met, but I was thinking about the night at the Bearded Squirrel and then afterwards when we went to that broken down amusement park."

Hunter's eyes wandered across the room when the whispers broke into our conversation.

"—how shitty my life is now. I used to play football in high school for Chrissakes. First team all county. We were state champs. I thought I'd get to play ball with my kids one day. Now I can't walk."

"Hey Hunter?" I stroked his arm soothingly. He was shifting around in his seat, an uneasy grimace on his face.

"Yeah. Mmhm. The amusement park."

"Remember how we threw the rocks at the old booth game and it fell down?" I asked. I smiled ostentatiously for him. It had been a fun night, and I wanted him to remember it. Hopefully that would get Hunter to think about happier times instead of the results looming over us.

"What about it?"

"Well, I'm happy you won Bernie for me at the carnival last week. I'm glad we finally got a chance to play some real—"

"—can't provide for them. We're up shit creek in debt. Last week they took my car. They're coming for the house next. Disability ain't comin' close to makin' the payments."

I looked over across the room, feeling a little uneasy myself. The man had started sobbing quietly into his hands. When I turned back to Hunter, the muscles on his neck were tense and he was breathing heavily.

I tried to get him to meet my eyes but he was fixated on the scene across the room. "Talk to me," I pleaded. "Please."

"—used to look up to me. I had a job. Construction. Now I can't even walk, forget about working. I'm a burden on them. Now with this damn MS I'm useless. What have I got to live for?"

Hunter bolted upright, almost knocking over the chair. Then he turned on his heel, his body a tight rod of tension, and stormed out.

I sat stunned.

"Wait!" I yelled, but he was already through the doors. I shot up to my feet and followed.

When I got outside he was in the parking lot, pacing back and forth. I sprinted to him, heart pounding and reached for his wrist. His forearm was a tight bundle of muscle, but he didn't pull away.

Hunter stopped pacing and shook his head. I paused to catch my breath, but I didn't let go of his arm. His entire body was trembling.

"Sorry," he said. "I just can't listen to that guy anymore."

"It's going to be okay," I said, panting.

"No, it's not," he said. He pointed angrily at the doors of the clinic. "Did you see him? Hear how miserable he was? That could be me in a year!"

"It won't be like that."

"Can you promise me that?"

"I . . . " I knew I couldn't do that. No one could promise that, but I had to believe that it would be okay. I tried again. "No matter what happens, I'll be there with you. We can deal with it together. You know that!"

"What if we can't?"

Frustration clenched in my chest. What was he talking about? I thought we had worked this out. Why was he talking this way now?

The words poured out of his mouth. "Even with you by my side maybe I can't deal with it. Maybe I'm not the guy you think I am. Maybe I won't be able to handle finding out that I'm gonna end up being crippled or worthless or dead in a few months. Maybe I'm just too *weak* . . ."

He looked away from me, his face red.

A knife sliced through my heart, making every breath difficult to take. Was he just saying those things because he was scared or did he really mean them? Hearing those words come from his mouth hurt more than anything he could have said at that moment.

A bubbling fury rose in my chest, ready to explode.

"STOP IT!" I yelled, stomping my foot. "How can you even *say* those things? If it wasn't for you, I'd probably be at the bottom of a lake right now."

My vision was starting to get blurry and my face wet, but I didn't care. If people passing through the parking lot wanted to watch me cry, so be it.

Hunter didn't say anything, his fists working at his side.

I hit him on the chest as tears beaded and fell down my face, trying to drive every word into his heart. "If it wasn't for you, I'd still be numb and empty because of what happened to my parents. You were the only one could drag me out."

He grabbed at my hands to stop me from hitting him. "Lorrie, stop . . ."

I wrenched my hands away. I wasn't done yet.

"If it wasn't for you, I'd still be hiding in bed, afraid of the world, afraid of everything. Every time I fell, it was your strength that picked me up off the floor so don't you *dare* say you're weak. You're the strongest person I've ever met!"

My lungs felt like they were about to burst. I angrily wiped my eyes and shook the tears off of the back of my hand. Pursing my lips, I stared at him defiantly, daring him to challenge what I had said.

Hunter stared right back at me, his chest heaving. At first I thought he was going to argue with me, but the intensity in his eyes faded away into sorrow.

I knew that he'd been fighting this battle for a long time before I came into his life and I knew that it wasn't easy for him. I also knew that he was a lot stronger than he gave himself credit for. Maybe no one had ever told him that, maybe he just needed to hear it from me, but I knew that he had it in him.

I took a few deep breaths to steady myself. Then I continued more softly. "I know this is your choice to make, but if finding out the results of this test will help the doctors treat you better, then I think you should go back in there. Whatever happens, I know you're strong enough to face it."

Hunter puffed up his cheeks and blew out a long breath. "You still think I'm strong?" he asked, "Even after you've seen how scared I am?"

"There's nothing wrong with being scared. I'm scared too. Maybe I'm even more scared than you, but someone I love once told me that *when you're in a fight being afraid of getting hit is worse than the hit itself.*"

He shook his head in disbelief and ran a hand through his hair. Then he turned to look at me again before lifting his face to the sky and sucking in a deep breath through his teeth. When he exhaled, it was like all the tension had left his body.

Hunter wrapped his arms around me. I let myself sink into him for a moment, before I threw my arms around him too and hugged him close to me. We had to face this battle together.

When we finally untangled ourselves from each other, a small smile cracked on his lips and he met my eyes sheepishly.

"I gotta be careful what I say around you," he said. "Else you're gonna use it against me someday."

I choked out a laughed, still sniffling and slapped his arm lightly.

Hunter smiled and looked down at the asphalt, lost in his thoughts for a few moments. After a while, he looked at me, his eyes sharp and clear. "Thanks for not letting me do something stupid again. I know it's been difficult for you."

I shook my head. "It's okay. That's what we're here for right? To save each other from doing stupid things? You've saved me a few times already, so I guess it's my turn now."

He nodded slowly, a thoughtful expression on his face.

"Let's go back inside. They're probably gonna call me in soon."

When we got back inside the clinic we each spent a few minutes in the bathroom, cleaning ourselves up.

Hunter and I sat down after we'd straightened ourselves out. We waited for his name to be called. The old lady and the guy in the wheelchair were gone; they must've been called inside already. A few minutes later a doctor cracked the door open.

"Hunter Jensen?"

I squeezed Hunter's hand and we got up and walked over to the doctor together. The doctor had to be at least sixty. His hair was completely white, and his thick black rectangular glasses covered his wrinkled eyes.

We followed him to the back. The room was like any other doctor's room, with posters of veins and nerves up on the walls. The beige exam table had seen better days. Its cushioning looked lumpy and uneven and the wood laminate on its base was chipped. Hunter eyed it with a distaste and sat down in one of the waiting chairs. I sat down next to him.

"Hello Hunter," the doctor said. "I'm Dr. Miller and I'll be interpreting your MRI results today."

He gave us a small smile, then pressed a button on the wall behind the counter. The light box hummed on. Apparently Dr. Miller wasn't one for small talk. Hunter didn't say anything, but he did nod. I watched him carefully to see if he was still okay, but I couldn't read his expression.

I thought I was ready and his mini freakout from earlier had distracted me from my own emotions, but now I was feeling the full weight of what was about to happen. When Dr. Miller produced an extra large manila envelope, I didn't feel prepared.

"I've received the scans back from the test center and had a chance to read them," he started. He pulled out the films and began put them onto the light box.

Hunter fixated on the images, as if he was trying to interpret them himself.

"Now, your primary care doctor over in Illinois sent me your records. The notes said that you sustained physical trauma to the head recently from 'cage-fighting.' Is that correct?"

Dr. Miller raised an eyebrow at Hunter. I held my breath.

"Yeah." Hunter replied, tearing his eyes away from the MRI scans.

"Well, I'll cut to the chase. Your doctor was worried about extremely rapid progression of your MS symptoms as a result of the physical trauma you suffered, but the good news is we've avoided the worst case scenario."

We both let out a breath and I gave Hunter's hand a small squeeze. We were going to be okay.

Dr. Miller cleared his throat and continued, pointing to a few spots on the MRI film. "However, it does appear you have some new lesions on your spinal cord and brain since your last scan."

The hairs on the nape of my neck rose and my palms grew sweaty. What? I thought we had avoided the worst case scenario.

"So what does that mean?" Hunter asked, frowning.

"Well, even though we've avoided the worst case scenario, these lesions are worrying, and could make your next flare-up a lot worse."

"How much worse?" Hunter asked.

"I can't say. But I would strongly advise you to refrain from continuing to fight. Sustaining lesions like this is not good for your long-term prognosis with this disease."

I looked to Hunter's face, but his brows were furrowed and he didn't seem to register my concern. Dr. Miller's words echoed in my mind, but I was only slowly starting to understand what he meant. Hunter was okay for now, but his next episode could be a lot worse if he didn't stop fighting?

Hunter squinted at the scans on the lightbox. "So if I stop fighting, will it prevent another attack?"

"It would certainly help a great deal, but there are no guarantees. MS is an autoimmune disease. Your body is attacking itself and it's very unpredictable."

Hunter clammed up and looked down at the linoleum tiles on the floor. I could tell he was tense. He looked the same as when he stormed out of the clinic earlier. I stroked his hand gently, trying to provide whatever comfort I could.

Even if Hunter did everything he could to be healthy, his MS could still knock him down at any moment. It made any preventative action he took seem trivial. I was starting to understand why he felt so helpless.

"Is that all?" Hunter grunted. I could tell he was upset, but I didn't know how to make it better.

"Yes, that's all we can tell from the MRI. Treatment-wise, we don't need to make adjustments. Have you been continuing with your injections regimen?"

Hunter nodded.

"Other than that, make sure you stay healthy and call the clinic immediately if you notice any new symptoms. Do you have any other questions?"

"Nah, thanks doc." Hunter stood up and I followed his lead. Dr. Miller walked us out to the waiting area in front while Hunter seemed deep in thought.

After the doctor parted ways with us and Hunter had completed his post-visit paperwork at the front desk, I followed him outside in silence.

It seemed like we had avoided the worst case scenario, but there was still a terrifying cloud hanging over our head. Beyond that, we hadn't even started talking about Hunter's fighting. Would he be willing to give that up to stay healthy? I didn't know, but what I did know was that it was a sensitive topic.

When we got to Hunter's car we both sat down inside without a word. Hunter stared out the windshield without putting his key into the ignition. I thought about what to say to him, opening and closing my mouth several times. What could I even say though?

Hunter saved me by speaking first.

"Fighting was the one thing that made me feel alive," he said, still looking out the front of the windshield.

I reached over and put a hand on his thigh to let him know that I was listening. His fighting was clearly a sensitive topic for him.

"After I got kicked out of ROTC, I was fucking lost. I'd been working at it for so long that when I realized it was over, I was outta control. Fighting gave me something to focus on."

He turned to me, his eyes shining and intense.

"It was like a drug. I had boxed and wrestled a lot in high school, so it was like returning home for me. It was something I knew, something I had control over when everything else in my life was so fucking outta control."

Listening to him talk like that made hot tears bead in my eyes. I knew how he felt. I knew what it was like to feel weak and helpless and lost. When you're in that situation, the only thing you could do was look for something to hang onto so you wouldn't drown.

"Yeah, I guess drawing is like that for me," I whispered.

Hunter might have found something he could control in fighting but I didn't know if I could watch him step into the cage again after what Dr. Miller had said. Even if it was the only thing that made him feel alive, how could I stand by and watch him slowly kill himself?

I took a deep breath. I had to tell him how I felt. "I don't know if—" I started, my voice cracking.

He shook his head, "I knew it was stupid, fighting with my condition, but I couldn't stop. I didn't even know *how* to stop."

He reached over and smeared my tears off with his thumb.

"Lorrie, I'm done with all of that bullshit," he said.

"Wh—what?" I mumbled.

"First I thought I needed the Air Force. Then when that was over, I thought I needed the fighting. But none of that shit matters. The only thing I need is you. I know I gotta face my disease the right way, not just for me, but for us. I can't keep doing it the fucked-up stupid way I was doing it before."

I watched him in disbelief. "Do you really mean that?"

"Yeah. I love you. I know how much it would hurt you if something awful happens because I'm being a dumbass."

Hunter leaned over and kissed me, his lips warm and comforting against mine. We finally pulled apart.

"I love you too," I said after, holding back tears. Seeing the way Hunter was handling this made my heart swell with pride. I was right about him. He was the strongest person I had ever met.

Chapter Sixteen
CLINT

The next day, Hunter seemed in a better mood and it was contagious. Even though some of what Dr. Miller had said was worrying, it was pretty good news overall, especially considering how much worse it could have been. Hunter spent the morning working on the dining room. It seemed like his new healthier attitude towards his condition was giving him new energy. I even felt excited about my session with Dr. Schwartz scheduled for the next day. I couldn't wait to tell her about everything that had happened since our last talk.

In the afternoon, he invited me to go check out the gym the operator at the carnival had recommended. I accepted, hoping he was going to keep his word about not fighting, and soon we were in his car and on our way.

Soon, we were driving into the town center. I turned to Hunter. "No more detours to get our fortunes told, okay?"

"You don't wanna check in with our friend Trinity?" he asked, smirking.

I shook my head until my hair was in my eyes.

"Fine. Not sure we'd have time anyway. This gym is only open for another couple hours."

"Okay. Did you call to let them know you were coming? What's your plan with this anyway?"

Hunter laughed. "I called, yeah. The guy on the phone was pretty short with me, though. He seemed cool with me coming in but definitely wasn't promising anything."

I shrugged. "I guess that makes sense. So what are you thinking you're going to do there?"

"I dunno. Just wanna check it out I guess. Get a feel for the place. I don't wanna fight like I was before or anything, but maybe it would be a good spot to work out. Or maybe I can work there. Gotta find some way to start paying for myself sooner or later."

"Fair enough," I said. I was skeptical of anything coming from this, but Hunter taking steps toward a plan for a long-term future was promising enough for me.

A few minutes later, Hunter pulled over and parked in front of a sign that read "Clint's Gym." The place looked like it hadn't changed since the nineties.

"So you think you talked to Clint?" I asked after we'd gotten out of the car.

Hunter looked up at the sign. "I'm guessing. Guy had the voice of someone who yells a lot."

"Maybe you'll be yelling a lot too when you start coaching," I said.

I hadn't been sure how serious I was, but Hunter took me at my word. "Yeah, maybe."

He seemed to be lost in thought as we walked to the entrance, so I kept my mouth shut. We got to the glass door, opened it, and went inside.

My first impression centered on how rundown the place was. The second was that it reminded me a lot of Hunter's gym in Studsen. Bigg's had some more recent music, maybe, and there seemed to be more wrestling, but that was about it. The two places were pretty close.

Hunter began surveying our surroundings the instant we were inside. Seemingly in a trance, he made his way past the unoccupied front desk and to the entrance to the gym area, where the sound of leather hitting leather could be heard.

When we walked in, the pungent smell of disinfectant practically punched me in the face. How on earth were they using so much of the stuff? I looked around and saw a bucket in the corner. Holy cow.

Hunter seemed unfazed by the smell or anything else. His eyes scanned the room, taking in all the activities being performed.

There were almost a dozen people in all working out in various stations. To our right we found a series of small and big punching bags being hit by fighters of various sizes. To our left were a couple of mats. One of them was in use, and the two wrestlers seemed to be drilling a move where one of them would try to grab the other guys legs and the other guy tried to stop him from getting a good grip.

"What are they doing over there?" I asked Hunter.

Hunter looked over briefly. "Takedown defense," he answered, before screwing up his face in skepticism. "Kinda."

I watched as the guy attempting the takedown was successful and nodded. Logical enough name. When I turned to ask Hunter what he meant by "kinda," I saw he had turned his attention to the room's centerpiece.

It was the sparring ring. The thing looked even older than the one in Bigg's. Its ropes were fraying on the far side especially, the wood along the side was chipped, and it even looked like the floor was slightly uneven. Nevertheless, two fighters—who looked to be about sixteen—were in the ring with helmets, fighting each other under the instruction of a third man. I didn't need to be told the third man was Clint.

He wore a pressed, crisp maroon polo and had his nearly white hair cropped close to his head. His tall, thin frame bounced around the mat like that of a young man, and his voice barked instructions with startling intensity. If I had to guess, I would say he was in his late sixties, if only because I couldn't imagine him being any older given how spry he was.

One of the boxers appeared to make him so irritated he pulled him aside and stepped in his place, showing him the correct footwork. He threw some practice punches on the other fighter and had the other fighter throw some punches back to demonstrate the technique.

"Son, you can throw 'em faster," he barked. "You won't hit me."

The other fighter obliged, though Clint was right. He wasn't getting touched.

"Alright," he bellowed in his raspy voice. "Again."

He backed up and watched them. After another couple of minutes of sparring, he finally acknowledged us. "You the guy on the phone?" he called, keeping his back to us.

I looked to Hunter, who had been observing carefully. "Yeah," he answered.

Clint turned to us now for a moment, looking over his shoulder. "I'll be with you in a minute."

Hunter nodded but said nothing, since Clint had already turned back to the action in the ring. He appeared to be a man of few words.

The fighters took a break a few minutes later, and Clint got down from the ring to greet us. After introductions and some handshakes, he got right to business. "So what can I do for you?" he asked.

Hunter pursed his lips for a moment, then shrugged. "Well, I just wanted to check the place out and see if there was anything I might be able to help with."

"Did you now?" Clint asked, his eyebrows raised and a small smirk on his face. "Find anything? Been meanin' to get that ring painted up . . ."

His tone was skeptical bordering on humorous, but Hunter soldiered on. I had always admired his ability to let it roll off his back when someone wasn't taking him seriously. "I was actually just watching those two kids wrestle," he replied.

The smirk left Clint's face and was replaced by his previous seriousness. "And?"

"I think I could probably help them out."

Clint squinted. "You mean coach them?"

Hunter nodded. "Yeah. Their technique has a lot of holes, and I figure with the way the fight game's going these days you're going to have a lot of kids who wanna do MMA. If you wanna do mixed martial arts, you better have good wrestling or someone is gonna take you down and kick your ass. Doesn't matter how good your boxing is if you're on your back."

"I've seen some of this cage fighting stuff," Clint said, definitely interested now. "You know all that, then?"

Hunter smiled. "Yeah, I know it."

"How do I know you know it?"

I pursed my lips. Was Hunter going to have to fight again?

"Got anyone here you think could wrestle me?" Hunter asked.

The air left my lungs. It looked like he would.

"Right now?"

"Why not?"

Clint shrugged and looked around. "What do you weigh?"

"About two-ten."

"Alright. Only guy I have is Yevgeny, but he's probably closer to two-fifty and knows his wrestling. If you really want to, have at it."

My eyebrows shot up. Did he say two-fifty? That was like NFL football player big. I grabbed Hunter's arm to tell him I didn't think this was a good idea, but I was too late.

"Yeah," Hunter said. "Let's do it."

My stomach dropped. We all went over to one of the free wrestling mats, then Clint went to go get Yevgeny from where he was working on a punching bag. The boxers working around the gym got wind of what was going on and gathered round the mat before Yevgeny had even arrived.

Yevgeny finally came, followed closely by Clint. Yevgeny was a college-aged guy about the same age as me and Hunter, and enormous. He wasn't anywhere near as ripped as Hunter was, but he was bigger. The white undershirt he wore was at least a double XL and it still fit tight around his arms. His short hair sat atop a thick brow, and his expression signaled nothing but confidence.

Hunter had taken off his sweatshirt and was now wearing an undershirt and jeans. He seemed to be sizing Yevgeny up, undisturbed by what he saw.

"Hunter," I whispered, grabbing his arm. "Do you think think this is a good idea?"

He patted my hand and gently freed himself from my grasp. "Yeah, it'll be fine. It's just a friendly spar and it's wrestling so they're not gonna hit me. I meant what I said when I told you I'm serious about taking care of myself. We won't get too rough."

I hesitated, but I didn't say anything else. It didn't make me happy, but I couldn't set limits for Hunter. I had to let him make his own choices.

With a final smile back at me, Hunter stepped onto the mat and waited for Yevgeny to do the same. Yevgeny stepped on with a wry smile on his face.

On Clint's signal, the two men crashed together. I watched Hunter's arms as they flexed, straining against his larger opponent. Even in his jeans, his butt looked amazing while he was bent down trying to get under Yevgeny's center of gravity.

It all happened in an instant. Hunter stood up straight, pulling Yevgeny toward him quickly. Then he swiveled his hips around and turned, his back bulging as he brought Yevgeny forward until he tripped on Hunter's trail leg and fell down to the mat on his back. Yevgeny's eyes bulged in surprise as Hunter came crashing down on top of him for the pin.

I didn't know much about wrestling, but that looked impressive.

The room went silent as the gym's fighters watched their best get put on his back. Clint's voice thundered through the quiet and brought everyone back to reality.

"Very nice," he cried. "Again!"

I watched with lips pursed as Hunter and Yevgeny got up to wrestle again. The two men came together at Clint's signal, and grappled back and forth for a while, but eventually Hunter was able to pull the same move. This time there was some appreciate murmuring from the fighters around the ring.

"Alright," Clint said. "One more time. Yevgeny, are you gonna let him keep doing the same move on you?"

Yevgeny's face was red with a combination of embarrassment and exertion. He was scowling when the two men came together for a third time. I held my breath as I watched the now familiar grappling, hoping Hunter could pull off the same move. He seemed to really want this job with Clint and coaching would definitely be a more productive use of his fighting skills than the MMA he had been doing before.

This time, when Hunter stood up Yevgeny didn't go with him. Instead he seemed to disengage from Hunter's grasp and come at Hunter in a more controlled manner.

Hunter had the answer, though, as he faked briefly in one direction and then spun around to Yevgeny's back, wrapping both arms around his waist.

The larger man looked confused for a moment. Hunter grunted and bent his knees before leaning back and picking Yevgeny up off the ground with a loud cry. The two came down to the mat with a thud, Hunter on top. The impact was so forceful I felt the floor shake.

"Holy shit!" one of the fighters gathered round the mat yelled.

Clint whistled. "That's all I need to see. Son, you want a job, let me know."

My heart leapt. I watched Hunter's expression on the mat. He looked as happy as I had ever seen him. We spent another hour at the gym and Hunter gave a few more tips to some of the guys. I watched from the sidelines, enjoying my view of him working up a sweat.

Hunter was still in a great mood on the drive home. As I sat in the car looking out the window, I finally understood why he had held onto fighting as long as he had. He loved it, and he was very good at it. I was just glad that coaching could be a step toward him finding a productive use for that passion.

Chapter Seventeen
PROGRESS

The next day, I found myself in the waiting room outside of Dr. Schwartz' office. It had been two weeks since our last session. So much had happened. I wondered what she would make of it.

Dr. Schwartz interrupted my thoughts when she came into the waiting area. She waved at me and I got up, following her through the heavy mahogany doors to her inner office. Even though I couldn't quite place it, something felt different. The light coming through the window shades was brighter and the clock on her desk didn't seem nearly as menacing as it had before.

We settled down, me on the tan couch and Dr. Schwartz beside her desk. She looked at me, her face neutral, waiting for me to begin.

I settled back into the couch and thought about how to start. The last time I had spoken to Dr. Schwartz, I had barely been able to get out of bed. My relationship with Hunter was in shambles and it seemed like we were both doomed to be lost forever. Now things were different.

"I don't even know where to start . . ." I said, trailing off.

How could I even begin to tell Dr. Schwartz everything that had happened since the last time I was here? I felt like a completely different person. It was probably best to start with the most important change. "Hunter and I had a chance to talk."

She raised an eyebrow and wrote on her pad. "What did you talk about?"

For the next few minutes, I gave her a rundown of Hunter showing up at my aunt's place and how we agreed to work things out. I told her about Hunter's MS, how he promised to stop hiding things from me and his test results.

When I was done, she finished up writing some notes on her pad and looked at me over her glasses. "So it appears you're recovering well."

That phrase. *Again*. I shuddered as I went back to the first letter I'd received from Marco when I was still at Arrowhart.

My therapist seemed to notice my reaction. "Is something wrong?"

"That phrase," I said, shaking my head. "Marco used it in the letter he sent me at Arrowhart."

"What phrase?"

"'I hope you're recovering well,'" I quoted. "For some reason that stuck with me. Like of course I'm not. How could I be? What does that even mean?"

Dr. Schwartz wrote furiously on her pad. "This phrase," she started. "Does it occur to you in other places? Dreams, maybe?"

I considered this for a moment. "I guess I notice when people say it . . . but it hasn't been showing up in any of my nightmares, no."

Her eyebrows arched up. "Nightmares?"

"Dreams. I don't know."

"Does Marco appear in these dreams?"

I pursed my lips. "Sometimes."

"And how does he appear?"

"I don't know. Usually he just pops up out of nowhere." I said, looking around the room instead of at her.

"What does he do?"

I shook my head slowly. "He attacks me. Tries to hurt me."

"Are you afraid of him hurting you?"

"In the dream? Yeah, definitely. In real life? No. I know he's in a maximum security prison. He's not getting out of that."

She clicked her pen a few times. "Do you have any theories about why Marco has shown up in your dreams? Did you ever write him a letter?"

"I did, actually. Write him, I mean. I don't know why he would show up in my dreams so much lately. I guess it's just been bothering me, wondering why he did it."

"Did you ask him?"

"Yes."

She noted this on her pad and then sat silent, listening for me to speak again. Eventually I continued on.

"I hope he answers. It feels like that's the missing piece for me to recover. Finding out why."

I fell silent and waited for her to be the one to talk next. As far as I was concerned, I'd said all I needed to.

It took a while, but eventually she relented. "How do you feel about the way you've handled the death of your parents since the last time we met?"

That wasn't what I'd been expecting. "I don't know, pretty good I guess. I think sending that letter to Marco was a good idea. Thank you for the suggestion."

I'd expected her to smile at that, but she kept her face neutral. "You're welcome. What are you expecting from that letter?"

"An answer, I hope."

"And if you don't get the answer you're hoping for?"

I shrugged. "Back to the drawing board. I don't know yet how I'm going to recover if I don't know why it happened. Honestly I'm not sure I can. It's just such a mystery."

She nodded and wrote some more before putting her pen down. "What does recovery mean to you, Lorrie?"

"What do you mean?"

"Earlier we talked about how Marco used that word and how it's stuck with you."

"Right," I said, squinting as I tried to understand what she was getting at.

"So what does that word mean to you? It might seem obvious but I just want to know what you think."

It felt like she was trying to trick me. I fell back deeper into the couch and considered what she was asking. I'd been told since my mom died that I was supposed to be trying to recover. Now she was asking me what that meant?

"I don't know," I said carefully. "What do you think?"

"It's not about what I think, and I'm not trying to confuse you here. Let's just talk through this. What does recovery mean?"

I sighed. "Get back to normal?"

"Good," she said, nodding. "How much do you think you have recovered to this point? Based on that criteria."

Even though I opened my mouth to answer, I had nothing. After a moment during which I felt stupid, I closed it and thought about what to say.

How could I even answer that question? Was my life back to normal? Definitely not. Normal people didn't have nightmares about their mother's murderer.

But how close was I, even? The more I thought about it, the more muddled my mind became.

Everything had changed with Hunter, basically. Our relationship was going pretty well, but it couldn't exactly be called "normal." He was such a unique person dealing with his own issues, and I hadn't fully gotten over mine either. Maybe there was no normal for us. Maybe . . .

"I can tell you're having trouble with that one," Dr. Schwartz said, interrupting my musing. "But that's fine. It's a very complex issue. I'd like you to think about that over the coming weeks and we can talk about it more at our next session."

She stood up and held out her hand for a handshake. I rose and took it unsteadily. This wasn't normal for her. For once, she was even smiling.

"I think that you're making terrific progress," she said. "Whether it's toward recovery or something else, it seems the future is certainly looking up for you Lorrie. I want you to know that I'm proud of the work you've done toward building your future. It's very brave."

It was a little surprising that she seemed so positive now, after the things she had said before. I looked to her with my eyebrow raised, but she kept smiling as she showed me to the door. There was no harm in it, I figured. If she thought I was making progress, even it wasn't toward something in particular, that was good enough for me. Maybe I even agreed with her.

Chapter Eighteen
AN INVITATION

I woke up at my desk from an impromptu nap feeling like I was missing something. It was Friday, and I'd been working on a picture for Hunter in my room after an early lunch. I had only intended to rest my eyes, but I'd definitely been out for a while, and while I couldn't remember my dream I had a feeling it had been intense. Even though my therapy session with Dr. Schwartz the previous day had raised some questions, overall I was feeling quite good today. Maybe she was right, I just had to reflect on what happened with Marco and my parents and I would get close to recovering.

Still groggy, I sat back in my chair and tried to get my bearings. I looked down at the desk. A half-finished sketch of Hunter captaining a boat lay in the spot my head had been a moment earlier. The kittens were scattered around the boat, and some of them even wearing silly sailor hats.

It was an amusing picture. When I was done, I was pretty sure Hunter would get a kick out of it.

I looked at the clock while stifling a yawn. Already almost three o'clock. Wow, time had flown. As I stood up, I glanced out the window and saw the mailman leaving.

Perfect timing. Since I had submitted my portfolio, I had been making a point of checking the mail every day in case there was news about my entry. Hoping this might be the day, I rushed down the stairs and out the front door.

A large white envelope was waiting for me in the mailbox. I pulled it out and saw it had my name on it.

The envelope was from the Illinois Arts Council. I hadn't been this excited by a piece of mail since my acceptance to Arrowhart.

Leaving the rest of the mail in the box for the time being, I tore the envelope open and pulled out the letter.

> *Dear Lorrie,*
>
> *Congratulations! You have been invited to exhibit at the Illinois Arts Council's Convention for Undergraduate Students at Arrowhart College.*

I stopped reading there and yelled out in triumph. This was it! I had made it to the next round. Excited to explore the rest of the envelope's contents, I gathered up all the mail and ran back inside the Perkins house.

I opened the door and rushed to the living room. Hunter was working in the dining room, but my aunt was nowhere to be seen. Uncle Stewart was at work and the kids were at school.

"I got invited to exhibit!" I yelled, jumping up and down.

Bones and Frida came out from some corner to see what all the commotion was about. I took a seat on the couch, threw the rest of the mail on the coffee table, and began to read my letter from the Illinois Arts Council again.

I was being invited to exhibit a week from this upcoming Saturday. In order to win the award, I had to exhibit. The Council would pay for hotel accommodations for the weekend. As a finalist, I needed to be prepared to talk for ten minutes about my portfolio for the judges.

Taking a deep breath, I scanned to the end of the page and then put the letter aside to flip through the glossy brochure that had been included. There was a long list of art schools that would be represented at the convention.

This could be a huge opportunity to network with a lot of great places. My mind spun as I thought about the best way to take advantage of the chance to meet all these people.

"What was all that yelling about?" Hunter asked, wiping his hands as he came in from the dining room.

"I'm a finalist!" I said excitedly. I grabbed the letter and stood up from the couch to show him.

It took him a second to register before his gray eyes brightened. "For the art competition?" he asked.

I nodded happily.

"Oh wow Lorrie, that's awesome!"

He took my letter in one hand and hugged me close to him with his other. I threw both arms around his torso and gave him a big squeeze.

"Wow, this thing's coming up. I'll have to make plans to go with you. I've never been to an art exhibition, but it's probably cool, right?"

I shrugged. "I've never been to one either, but probably."

"It's totally going to be one of those places where people are all like 'I do say, Richard, what a marvelous piece,'" Hunter said, slipping into a ridiculous posh English accent. He lowered his voice. "'Too right, too right my boy. Simply splendid. Such *emotive* brush strokes.'"

I giggled. "Wow, you know so much about art."

He shrugged sheepishly and handed the letter back. "I dunno, I'm guessing they would probably talk about brush strokes for paintings. Right?"

"Sure," I said with a laugh.

Just then my aunt came up from the basement. "What's all this fuss about?" she asked, coming into the room.

"I got invited to exhibit at Arrowhart next week for the art contest I submitted to." I said quickly.

Her face broke out in a big smile. "Oh my goodness! That's amazing!"

She took her turn with the letter and then began to flip through the brochure. "Lorrie there are a lot of art schools there. Do you think these are places you might want to apply?"

I looked at Hunter quickly before answering. "Yeah. I mean maybe. It's definitely worth checking out."

There was silence as my aunt continued to flip through the brochure. My heart pounded in my chest. This was so exciting, and yet my aunt's question had made the reality of going away for art school more real. Would Hunter come? If not, could we make a long-distance relationship work?

I bit my lip before smiling at him. He smiled back. We could cross that bridge when we got there. It was a long way off.

Chapter Nineteen
NEW BEGINNINGS

We made a lot of plans in the week leading up to the art convention. Aunt Caroline and Uncle Stewart were going to come up to Studsen with me to attend my exhibit. Hunter had just about finished his work on the dining room and started looking for short term apartments near the Perkins house.

He'd decided that since he would be staying in Eltingville with me at least for a few more months, he wanted to move out and get a place of his own. Even though my aunt tried to convince him to stay longer, we were pretty excited about looking around for a new place for him. Plus, Hunter having his own place would free up opportunities for fun *activities* we could engage in without having to worry about whose house we were in.

We had just found a fully furnished place that he liked a few blocks from the main highway and made an appointment to sign the lease the next morning. When we pulled into the driveway after seeing the apartment, Joel and Billy were chasing each other in the grass out front.

"You're back!" Billy yelled, running toward us.

Hunter nodded and waved at them.

"Are you taking the kittens with you when you move out?" Joel asked, catching up to his older brother.

Hunter picked Joel up and pretended to wrestle him, tousling his hair. "Yeah buddy, I think I will. The place is cool with pets, and I think the little guys have imposed on your mom and dad for long enough."

"Awww . . . " Joel and Billy said, almost in unison.

"Don't worry, I'll bring them by to visit when I come see Lorrie."

"Yay!" the boys sang. Billy latched onto Hunter's leg and tried to climb him like a tree.

I shook my head smiling. Those boys sure had their priorities straight. Hunter stayed behind to play with them while I headed into the house.

I was still smiling when I ran into my aunt in the kitchen. She turned around from stirring the large pot on the stove when I came in.

"Oh, there you are. Here, have a little snack. Dinner will be ready in an hour."

I opened my mouth to protest, but then the smell of chicken noodle soup reached my nose. Grabbing a small metal spoon from the drawer, I sat down and decided not to argue.

Aunt Caroline started cutting vegetables while I drank the soup. I watched her work. She was in a good mood, humming to herself.

"So, how was the apartment hunt today?" she asked.

"Pretty good, I think Hunter found one that he liked."

"You know he can stay as long as he wants, right?"

I nodded. "I told him that, but I think he'll feel better about living on his own somewhere."

"Well, you know the boys will be heartbroken with him and the kittens gone."

I laughed. "I'm sure he'll be around often enough that the boys won't mind."

"Hey now, it's not just the kids. I'll miss having him around to run errands, get groceries and cook breakfast for us too."

"Come on, Aunt Caroline, it won't be that bad. I'll help you do those things."

"Okay, if you say so. I'll hold you to that," she said. She turned and winked at me before wiping her hands on the kitchen towel and leaning back against the counter. "Are you excited about the convention tomorrow?"

"Yeah! I'm definitely excited. A little nervous I guess."

"That's normal, dear. When I was in college I nearly fainted in the middle of my final presentation for my public speaking class!"

I laughed. It was weird to think of a college aged Aunt Caroline. I pictured her hair in a scrunchie like I'd seen in the photo of her with my dad. "Wow. I definitely hope nothing like that happens."

"I'm sure you'll handle it better than I did. The most important thing is meeting all the representatives from these art schools. I imagine that will be more one-on-one than a giant crowd."

I considered this. "Yeah, though it would definitely be cool to win. I guess at this point it's already more than I could have hoped for, getting to meet people from these art schools and have a chance to have my work judged at a high level. I'm just going to try and enjoy it."

"I think that's a very good attitude, dear."

My aunt hummed cheerfully. When she noticed that my bowl was empty, she tutted. "Here I am talking your ear off and you must be starving. Would you like—"

Billy came in the front door. "MOM!"

Something was wrong. My aunt's eyes went wide and she dropped the ladle in her hand before bolting for the door. I followed right behind her, my heart in my mouth.

Billy waited just long enough for us to get to the door before running into the yard. When we got outside, it took a while to even understand what had happened. Billy came to a stop a few feet away from Hunter, who was on the ground. Joel was holding onto Hunter's hand, trying to drag him up.

"I'm okay. I'm okay," Hunter said. His words seemed fuzzy and indistinct and his eyes were unfocused. My stomach sank. I felt like I was going to be sick.

"What's going on here?" Aunt Caroline asked.

Joel let go of his hand and answered. "Hunter fell."

"It's okay," Hunter said. "Just a little scraped up."

He showed us his arm. An angry red rash covered a few inches of skin on his wrist. I looked at the frightened expressions on Joel and Billy's faces. This wasn't just a fall. Something wasn't right. My pulse pounded in my ears and the hair at the back of my neck stood up.

Hunter looked like a drunk man stumbling when he tried to stand up. He got up on one knee but when he tried to stand it buckled and he went down. I ran to him, taking his hand.

Even though I was trying to slow my breathing, my breath came in quick bursts. "What happened?" I asked, as calmly as I could.

His eyes were wide and panicked but he continued trying to stand up. "Shit. I'm sorry."

"Hunter, it's okay. Stay down for a minute. Tell me what's wrong."

"I'm okay. I'm okay. Just help me get up."

I eased myself under his armpit and strained to help him up. It was no use. His legs folded awkwardly under him and he was way too heavy to lift by myself.

I collapsed under him, panting.

A thin sheen of sweat covered his forehead. He gulped for air like a fish out of water. The doctor had said Hunter's next MS attack could be a lot worse. Was this it? From the look on Hunter's face, I could tell he was thinking the exact same thing. I was on the edge of panic, my throat dry and thick.

Whatever I felt at that moment, I needed to get myself under control. I turned to my aunt. Her eyes were wide with concern.

"I think we need to call an ambulance," I said, trying to keep my voice from shaking.

"No!" Hunter said. "No. It's fine. I just need to get to the hospital. I'm so sorry Ms. Perkins."

His face was red. He kept trying to get up but he couldn't. Watching him struggle sent hot spikes of pain searing through my heart. He was just as frightened as I was, maybe even more so.

My aunt looked at me for a second, her face full of questions, but thankfully she didn't ask any. She jumped into action right away. "I'll call Stewart and have him meet us at the hospital. Boys, get in the van."

Joel and Billy marched dutifully to the family's minivan, climbing into the backseat. Even though the situation looked bad, they had complete faith that their mother had things under control.

Once she was sure the boys had followed directions, my aunt turned to me. "Come on, help me move him."

I nodded numbly and put Hunter's arm around me again. Aunt Caroline took his other arm.

Even with the two of us, Hunter was very heavy. We half carried, half dragged him to the van. His legs dangled below him, unable to bear any weight. Eventually we got him into the middle row and put a seat belt around him. I sat in the middle row with him, while my aunt hurried around to the driver's seat and started the car. Soon we were on our way.

Hunter leaned back against the seat mumbling. His eyes looked sunken and feverish, but he was awake.

Aunt Caroline called my uncle as she made her way out of the subdivision. I watched Hunter to see if there were any changes in his condition, but he was barely lucid. More than anything, he looked exhausted. His normally bright face had a gray pall to it as he lay there trying to keep his head up. After a while, he started to nod off.

We were on the highway before I spoke. "Hunter has MS . . ." I managed to choke out. "I'm sorry we didn't tell you this earlier."

I blinked, trying to hold back the tears in my eyes. I knew that if I let myself feel the seriousness of this situation and start crying, I wouldn't be able to stop.

"I'm sorry dear, that sounds terrible," my aunt replied. "Does this happen often?"

"No," I said, a loud sob escaping from my lips. "At least, I don't think so. Definitely not this bad."

Now that I had said it out loud, I couldn't hold it in anymore. The tears streamed endlessly down my face.

Aunt Caroline stared at the road and nodded. I turned to look at Hunter again. He had fallen asleep and his chest was rising and falling slowly. For now, all the worries of the world had faded away.

But what would he think once he woke up?

Chapter Twenty
WAKE

The heart rate monitor beeped quietly, its eerie blue glow illuminating the room. I didn't know how much time had passed. Reaching into my pocket, I pulled out my phone. It had been fourteen hours since Hunter was admitted. The sun was probably coming up soon.

Aunt Caroline and Uncle Stewart had gone back home with the boys hours ago. There was no point in them being here anyway. Hunter was stable and my cousins needed to sleep. They were going to come back to check on us in the morning.

Hunter's chest rose and fell, his eyes darting around under his eyelids. Whatever he was dreaming about, I hoped it was good, because sooner or later he'd have to wake up to this nightmare. I let out a long sigh and rubbed my eyes. They were completely dry; I couldn't cry anymore. I was totally drained.

I heard shuffling on the bed and I bolted upright. Hunter was shifting around, his eyelids fluttering open.

"Lorrie?"

I scrambled to my feet and stood next to his bed. "Yes, I'm here."

His eyes were unfocused. He rubbed them with his hands, and for a second, I was worried about the IV on his arm falling out, but it stayed put.

"Where . . . " he started, before trailing off and looking around. His eyes fell on the needle in his arm. "FUCK!"

I stepped back, shocked by his sudden outburst. Adrenaline rushed through my veins.

"Shit. I'm sorry Lorrie. I'm just . . . fuck."

His eyes were becoming more clear and focused, but so was the pain on his face. I reached for his hand, gripping it tight.

"How long was I out for?"

"Maybe fifteen hours."

"I'm sorry," he said, his face red. "I didn't want to make things difficult for your aunt and uncle."

"You don't need to apologize. They're going to come back in the morning to see how you're doing."

"Shit, I gotta move out. We were supposed to sign that lease today. For that apartment."

"What? You don't need to worry about that right now. We'll find a different place. Just worry about getting better."

"Your aunt and uncle have let me stay in the house for so long already, I gotta move out soon."

"Hunter, stop it. You have to focus on getting better first."

"I—" he stopped when he saw the look on my face. I wasn't going to argue with him on this one.

"Stop it."

He took a deep breath.

"Okay fine. Can you get me some water?"

I handed him a bottle of water from the nightstand. He twisted the cap open and took a long deep gulp. For a while, we sat in silence.

A knock came at the door. It was followed by a doctor in a white coat coming into the room.

"Oh good" she said. "You're awake. Hunter, I'm Dr. Gallagher. How are you feeling?"

Hunter eyed the doctor with cautiously. "Alright. Little groggy."

Dr. Gallagher picked up the clipboard by Hunter's bed and looked through it, leafing through the pages.

"Good," she said. "Everything appears to be stable. How are your legs feeling?"

"I dunno, a little weak I guess, but I can feel them."

She nodded and lifted the sheets so that Hunter's legs were exposed. "I'm going to do a sensation test. Just tell me when you can feel me touching your legs okay?"

"Sure."

Dr. Gallagher pulled out a cotton ball from the metal cart at the side of the room and started touching it to different spots on Hunter's legs. He seemed to notice most of the times the cotton touched him. That was a good thing, right?

Then she moved on to poking him at various spots on his leg with a pin. He seemed to notice most of those as well, but when she asked him to lift his legs or wiggle his toes, he could barely muster any movement at all. Sweat beaded on his brow with the effort and I could tell he was getting upset.

After she was done, she started writing notes on her clipboard while Hunter and I watched. Hunter's face got progressively darker, as we waited for Dr. Gallagher to finish taking her notes.

"Well? What Is It?" Hunter demanded when It looked like he couldn't wait any longer.

"I'm sorry Mr. Jensen. You had an exacerbation of your MS, which seems to have affected the nerves to your lower extremities. The good news is your sensory nerves still have roughly seventy percent functionality."

"So how come I can't move my legs?" Hunter pointed angrily toward his lower half, taking shallow breaths.

"Your motor nerves, the ones that control your muscles, seem to be the most negatively affected.

That's the biggest factor in reducing your mobility at the moment."

Hunter's jaw clenched, his hands making fists by his side. I tried to meet his eyes, but he was staring off into the distance.

My stomach dropped. This couldn't be happening. Just yesterday he was fine and everything was going so well. I looked at Hunter but he just kept shaking his head like he was dazed. Why was this happening to him? He stopped fighting like the doctor told him too, so why had this happened now?

"For how long?" I asked.

Dr. Gallagher gave me a sympathetic look and then turned to Hunter. "It depends. Along with the motor nerves healing, there are issues with muscle degeneration since you'll be in a wheelchair for a while. Physical therapy can certainly help. With some patients PT is enough to restore full mobility in as little as six months. Other patients may never recover their mobility again."

My heart sank.

"The hospital can provide you with a wheelchair and we can refer you to a counselor to help you adjust to the . . . changes. You'll come back for a checkup in two weeks and if it's appropriate we'll get you started on a physical therapy regimen."

Hunter started rocking back and forth, not making eye contact with either of us.

Watching him like this was too much. I hugged his head close to my chest, kissing him on the forehead, and holding him to me. I wanted to cry but I bit back my sobs. If I let myself cry now, I wouldn't be able to stop.

When the doctor left, Hunter continued staring off into space and rocking himself. I held him and didn't say a word. What could I even say? After a few minutes, he finally stopped, seeming to snap out of it suddenly.

"Shit. What day is it?"

"What? I think it's Saturday?" I looked at him, confused.

His face sank. "Damnit. Your convention is today."

With everything that had happened, I had completely forgotten about it. He was right. The day of the convention had come. We had both been looking forward to going to it, but it didn't matter now.

"Oh yeah, I guess I can't make it,"

"No, what are you talking about?" he said, speaking quickly, his words tripping over themselves. "You can still make it if you leave now. When does it start? Like two? It's only seven in the morning right now."

"I don't care about the art convention, Hunter. I want to be here with you."

"You worked so hard for it. You can't miss your chance to exhibit."

"Hunter, I'm not leaving you to go to some art convention. How is that even a question?" It was irritating that he was so concerned about my stupid art convention when the doctor just told him that he might not be able to walk.

"It's fine, you heard the doctor, I'm stable now."

He looked anything but fine.

"Why do you want me to leave so badly?" I asked, a little hurt. My face felt heated.

"It's such a big opportunity. They'll have all the art schools there recruiting and stuff." Hunter pointed in the direction he must've assumed Studsen was going to be.

"I would have never won that competition if it wasn't for you, I probably wouldn't even have entered it. So stop talking, I've already decided. I'm not going without you."

Blood rushed to my ears and I felt a stinging in my eyes. Hunter let out a sigh, shaking his head.

"You said you thought you were gonna drag us down, but now I see that it's me," he said, his voice low.

"Don't say that. You know that's not true. We talked about this before, I *know* you're strong enough for this."

"It's different now. It's not just some far off thing that might happen to me, now it's fucking real."

He pounded the hospital bed with his fist. "I can't fucking walk, Lorrie!"

His words echoed in the room. Hunter grimaced, trying to hold a brave face, his eyes glistening. My heart was breaking into pieces but I didn't know what to say to make him feel better.

He continued before I could say anything. "Just leave me here. You need to go to the convention. Whatever happens to me, you can't give up your future for me."

"YOU ARE MY FUTURE!" I shouted. My lips trembled as warm wet streaks fell down my face.

Hunter's eyes went wide and then he looked down into his lap. I sobbed, my entire body shaking with emotion.

As I cried, rage boiled in my chest.

This isn't fair.

We were so close to our happy ending. Hunter didn't deserve this. He deserved so much more. I didn't know if I could give it to him, but it didn't matter. Hunter needed me now more than anything and I wasn't going to let him push me away. Even if it hurt me. Even if it broke me.

He sucked in a lungful of air and ran his hands through his hair.

I let myself cry, sobs coursing through my body. Hunter didn't say anything, his face somber.

After I cried myself out, I took a few deep shuddering breaths to steady myself. Then I looked into his soft gray eyes and started with a shaky voice. "Hunter, you're right. It is different now. Things have changed."

His eyes widened in surprise.

"But you haven't changed and I haven't changed. The way we feel about each other hasn't changed either. I promised to be by your side no matter what and I'm not leaving now. I love you, Hunter."

We sat there in silence, while my words hung in the air between us. He had been there for me, through so many things. He had absorbed so much of my pain and helped me heal, and now it was my turn to help him. I knew that I wasn't over my own issues yet, but I couldn't let them distract me from Hunter. He needed one hundred percent of me right now.

It was terrifying, and I could hardly even think about what our future together would be like now, but I wasn't going give up. Hunter never gave up on me, even when I pushed him away, even when I hurt him. I wasn't going to give up on him either.

Finally Hunter nodded slowly and let out a long breath.

"I'm sorry," he said, reaching for my hands and holding them to his lips. "I love you too. I'm so lucky to have you."

"No, I'm the lucky one," I choked out. "Just don't ever try to get rid of me like that again, okay?"

His gray eyes looked to me with piercing intensity and he squeezed my hand tightly. "I won't. I promise."

I stared deep into his eyes, hoping that we would be brave enough to face the challenges to come.

Chapter Twenty-one
CHANGES

I was in a hospital room. The white walls and searing bright lights stretched away into the distance. Hunter lay in the one bed at the center of the room and I sat in a chair maybe ten feet away from it. Wicked looking surgical instruments lay on a cart nearby.

What's going on?

Other than the chair, the hospital bed and the surgical cart, there was no other furniture in the room.

Something wasn't right. I didn't remember Hunter's hospital room being nearly this large. And why were there surgical instruments out? Hunter wasn't going into surgery.

I stood up from the chair and walked over to the bed. He was lying on his side, his back turned to me, his torso rising and falling slowly. Probably asleep.

Then I looked down to where his legs were. Blood seeped through the sheets, spreading rapidly until it soaked through the entire bottom of the bed. In a panic, I reached for the sheets and pulled them off. His legs were gone. Two bloody stumps were all that remained.

I opened my mouth to scream but nothing came out.

Hunter was stirring. He turned around slowly, but his face looked different. Icy chills shot through my veins from head to toe.

That's not Hunter.

Marco's face stared at me, his eyes wide and crazed. I stumbled backward and fell.

Then his mouth opened to speak.

"I hope you're recovering well."

My eyes sprang open. I sucked in lungfuls of air, trying to steady my breathing. My heart pounded against my ribcage and a slick layer of sweat covered my forehead.

I was still in a hospital room, but this one was normal sized and dimly lit. Hunter lay a few feet away from me, sleeping soundly. His eyes were closed and peaceful. This was definitely Hunter. His legs were fully intact, and one foot stuck out from under the sheet. My face was hot and I felt ashamed of myself. Why did I even need to check? I was like a kid scared of the dark.

Tears blurred my eyes and I wiped them away. The collar of my shirt was soaked with sweat, and my skin felt clammy.

I hope you're recovering well.

I shivered. The hospital's filtered air was too cold. It was okay. Hunter was going to be okay. We would be okay. I repeated it to myself like a mantra.

Except that he couldn't walk.

Clenching my jaw, I tried to prevent my lips from trembling even though I knew no one was watching me. Hunter might wake up at any second, and I didn't want him to see me crying. Wasn't I the one who wanted to be by his side to help him through this? Somehow I doubted that it would help him if he saw me in the middle of a panic attack.

It had already been a few days since Hunter had been admitted to the hospital. A number of other doctors had come and gone. They seemed to confirm what Dr. Gallagher had said about Hunter's legs. He might be able to walk again, but only after extensive physical therapy. In any case, there was no guarantee.

The reality of the situation was starting to sink in for me, and the nightmares came along for the ride. It seemed like every time I closed my eyes, some horrific vision greeted me, usually involving Marco in some way. The change in Hunter's condition seemed to have intensified my trauma over what happened to my parents at the worst possible moment. I knew I needed to be there for Hunter, but the nightmares were making it hard.

Other than his legs, Hunter was recovering well from the flare-up. They were trying to switch him to a different treatment. He'd still have to do injections, but it was a different drug. The good news was that despite the scary flare-up, the doctors said Hunter's disease was not progressing as aggressively as they had feared.

All in all, the news wasn't terrible. But it still didn't help me shake the horrible feeling at the bottom of my gut. I had promised Hunter that I would be there for him, but as the days wore on, and the nightmares ate at me, the more I wondered if I would be able to live up to that promise.

My fingers dug into the arms of the chair I was sitting in, making it a little slippery. Hunter's chest rose and fell peacefully.

His attitude seemed pretty good the past few days, cheerful even. When the doctors had offered him a reference to counseling services, he had insisted that he was okay with his situation and just wanted to get better. I didn't know if he was just pretending to be cheerful, or if he was just in denial about the seriousness of the situation. If he really was in denial, I was terrified of what might happen when he finally realized that even in the best case scenario, he wouldn't be able to walk for several months.

Footsteps interrupted my thoughts and a nurse came into the room. Hunter stirred at the noise and opened his eyes sleepily, rubbing them and stretching his arms out. The nurse looked at me curiously, before turning to Hunter.

"Good to see you're resting, I've got the discharge papers here and the wheelchair is right outside in the hallway. You can sign the paperwork, and whenever you're ready you can head out on your way."

Hunter pushed himself upright in the bed, a big sleepy grin stretching across his face. "Sweet, let's get going. Snorrie, you ready?"

I nodded and but I couldn't bring myself to smile back. We had been looking forward to Hunter being discharged today, but right now, I needed some time to compose myself.

"Yeah," I said, my voice cracked and I cleared my throat. "Just give me a second, I'm going to clean up a bit."

The nurse handed the clipboard to Hunter, while I walked out of the room. She didn't take her eyes off of me. Did I really look that bad?

In the hallway, I walked by the wheelchair that was meant for Hunter. The leather padding was old and cracked, but the chrome frame and plastic handles still gleamed like new. My eyes stung at the thought of Hunter in that chair. He was cheerful now, but would he still feel the same when he left the hospital?

I clenched my hands until I felt nail marks in my palms. Then I headed down the hall to the restrooms.

When I got to the ladies room and looked in the mirror, I could hardly recognize myself. My face was sunken and gray, my eyes bloodshot. How were we going to make this work? How could I possibly be strong enough for him when I was like this?

I could feel the tears welling up in my eyes, but I bit them back.

You need to be strong for Hunter. You're his anchor now.

The faucet squeaked when I turned it on and I splashed cold water on my face. He needed me. I couldn't let him down. And that was that.

A little less than an hour later, Hunter had finished all the paperwork and we went out the building's revolving door. He was still in a good mood and insisted on wheeling himself rather than letting me push him. I kept a fake smile on my face and let him do it, he seemed to have it under control.

We stopped at the car, and I opened the passenger side door for him.

"Thanks," he said. He flashed me a warm smile after hoisting himself into the front seat.

I folded up his wheelchair to put it in the back. "No problemo," I said, trying to keep my tone light. Even though I had to fake my cheerful tone, it did make me feel a little less depressed.

Once we were strapped in, we headed onto the freeway. We had the window down and the weather was starting to get a lot warmer. The breeze was making me feel better and I guess Hunter's positive mood was rubbing off on me too. Maybe it also helped that my nightmare about Marco was fading away.

"You know, I was thinking," Hunter said, turning to me.

"Uh-oh," I managed to tease in a playful tone.

He laughed before continuing, "I think it's time for me to get a job."

"A job? Now?"

"I dunno, I guess it would be nice to have something to do outside the house. The dining room just needs a layer of paint and then it's done."

"Okay, what did you have in mind?"

"Maybe I could still go work for Clint, you know, at the gym?"

"Oh."

"Don't worry, not like I'm gonna do anything crazy like spar or anything. I can do some coaching on the sidelines or whatever, maybe even just man the reception desk.

I looked over at his face, his eyes were round and excited. "Yeah, maybe that would be good for you."

Even though I wasn't sure if what he wanted was possible, it was nice to see that he was getting excited about something. It gave me some hope that things would turn out okay.

By the time we got back to the house, Hunter still seemed pretty cheerful. We stopped the car and I went to the back to take out the wheelchair. After I unfolded it, I put it next to the passenger side of the car and opened the door.

Hunter tried to lift himself into it by grabbing onto the arms but it would start rolling away whenever he put his weight on it.

"Here, I can help you with that," I said, stepping closer to hold it still for him.

"No, I got it," he said. He waved me away. Something in his tone made me stop. I wanted to help him but I knew that he didn't want me to treat him like he couldn't do anything himself.

After a few more tries, he was finally able to get himself onto the chair, but I could see the sharp line in his jaw. "Come on, let's go inside."

It was annoying that he refused to let me help, but I didn't say anything.

Before we even got to the front door, the boys zoomed outside. They must've been watching from the window. They cheered about Hunter getting back from the hospital and he humored them for a bit. At least my cousins didn't treat him any differently even though he was in a wheelchair.

Uncle Stewart followed them out, his tie still on, a can of soda in his hand. "Welcome back."

Hunter gave a curt nod. "Thank you, Sir." His jaw was tight again, and it was clear that he didn't want to say anything else.

My uncle grimaced awkwardly and shifted on his feet. We stood there for a moment, just watching each other, while Joel and Billy poked at the wheelchair. My aunt was probably too busy cooking to notice that we had come back.

Hunter looked down at his legs, before clearing his throat. "Thanks for letting me stay at your house longer. I really appreciate it."

"No problem at all, Caroline and I are happy to have you around," my uncle said.

Then we were back to awkward silence again.

"Should we go inside?" I asked, uncomfortable.

"Yeah," Hunter said. He rolled himself up to the front of the house, his wheelchair coming to a stop at the steps. He tried to get over the bottom step a few times, but it was clear that he wasn't going to be able to get over it, much less the next three steps leading up to the door.

He sat there, his face scrunched up. I walked over tentatively. I didn't want him to get upset like he had earlier when I tried to help him out of the car, but this time, there was no way he was getting into the house if we just left him there.

"Hey, can we help you with that?" I asked, trying to keep my voice as normal as possible.

Hunter stared at me intensely before his eyes darted to the steps and then my uncle.

"Um, yeah," he said, running his hand through his hair, and gritting his teeth.

I walked towards him and Uncle Stewart joined me after setting his soda down. Hunter's brows were furrowed. My uncle and I tried to find a good spot to grab the chair by, while Hunter stared ahead, not making eye contact with either of us. Finally we grabbed the wheels and lifted Hunter together. He just held onto our shoulders with his arms and grimaced.

Even though Uncle Stewart and I were the ones out of breath, Hunter's face was beet red. He mumbled a thanks to us before he rolled himself inside. I wanted to talk to him, but he was already gone.

My uncle went back for his soda, so I headed inside to find Hunter. I guessed he had gone straight to the guest room and I was right. Hunter had already moved himself to the bed by the time I got there.

He sat with his legs hanging off the side, his shoulders slumped forward, his lips tight in a thin line. Whatever good cheer he had left the hospital with was now long gone and he made no effort to disguise it. Seeing the pain in his eyes made my heart ache and I took a deep breath so I wouldn't cry.

It felt like it was so long ago that Hunter had told me that he would save us both. Now, he was the one who needed saving, but I didn't know how to do it.

"What's wrong?" I asked, regretting those words as soon as they came out of my mouth.

He laid down on the bed, and lifted his legs up with his hands. Then he rolled over and turned away from me. I bit my lip. I hated myself for asking such a dumb question but I didn't know what else to say.

"Nothing. I'm gonna get some rest. I think the move from the hospital wore me out."

"Okay," I whispered.

I turned to leave but stopped at the door. Even though I wanted to add something else, all I could think about was the tortured expression on his face. I needed more time to figure out the best way to help him.

Chapter Twenty-two
HELP

The next couple days passed by in a blur. My nightmares about Marco intensified and—on top of it all—he was starting to take up a lot of my conscious thoughts as well. I couldn't help but think that if he wrote back, with a reason for why he killed my mother, the nightmares would finally stop. I needed to focus on being there for Hunter, but Marco's intrusions into my thoughts were making it difficult.

I did my best to put a cheerful face on, but inside I was tied in knots. Seeing Hunter in a wheelchair was hard. Seeing how much he was struggling to adjust to it was even more painful. He tried to hide it, but when he thought I wasn't watching I kept catching him staring off into space.

Every day we fought to find normal, but the life we'd hoped for seemed to be slipping further and further away.

Late Wednesday morning, I came up with an idea that I hoped would make Hunter feel better about his situation. He had said he wanted a job at Clint's Gym, so maybe it would cheer him up if I took him there. Obviously he wouldn't be able to do the same activities he had done the last time we went, but he could still at least be around the fighters and maybe offer some tips on technique. More than anything, it would get him out of the house. Plus, doing something tangible for him would make me feel better about whether I was being as supportive as I needed to be.

When I came downstairs I went to the living room, where I assumed he would be. The couch was empty.

That was strange. I quickly checked the downstairs bathroom but saw that was empty as well. Nervous, I walked toward Hunter's room, hoping desperately there wasn't something else wrong with him. Maybe he was getting worse.

As I made my way to his door I heard a sound in the dining room. Brows furrowed, I changed course to see what was going on.

I entered the room to see Hunter sitting in his chair and using the gripper tool my uncle had bought for him to try to get a paint tray down from the top of a ladder. Uncle Stewart had just come home with the gripper the previous day.

"Hunter, what are you doing?"

He looked over at me briefly before going back to his attempt to grip the paint tray. There was already a can of paint and a roller on the floor next to him. "I'm gonna get some paint on these walls."

"Hunter, you don't have to do this. I'm sure my aunt and uncle understand—"

He shook his head before I was finished. "I *want* to do it, Lorrie."

I bit my lip, but said nothing. If he thought he could do this, I knew it wouldn't help to argue with him.

"Okay," I said, trying to make myself sound as cheerful as possible. "Let me get that tray for you."

I took a couple steps toward the ladder.

"NO!" Hunter boomed. My heart pounded in my chest and my cheeks felt heated. Why was he being so difficult?

He looked at me briefly and shook his head. "I can do this. I need practice with this thing if I'm going to be stuck in a wheelchair for a while."

I stood on my heels and watched him struggle to get the tray. The lip he was trying to grab the ladder by was pretty small, and since he was at an angle to begin with he had to get it exactly right if it was going to grip properly.

As he struggled with the gripper, his wheelchair slipped forward. He lunged dramatically to maintain his balance. The gripper caught the top of the ladder, tipping it.

The ladder fell with a loud crash.

I took a few steps toward Hunter's side, but stopped when I saw his expression.

He was okay, but I had never seen someone more frustrated in my life. His eyes were scrunched up and his jaw was set in a combination of anguish and rage. He shook for a moment, but didn't even yell.

He stared at the ladder and I stared at him for several seconds, neither of us making a move. Then I stepped tentatively toward the ladder.

"Don't touch it," Hunter rasped. "I got this."

"Let me help," I offered, bending towards the ladder.

"I SAID DON'T TOUCH IT!"

I froze, then straightened up and turned to face him. My heart beat loudly in my ears. A tense silence hung in the air, and I didn't want to be the one to break it.

Hunter saved me from having to. "Please leave," he said through his teeth. "I can handle this. Sorry for the noise."

I took a deep breath, trying to stop myself from screaming. "Hunter, what's your problem? I'm trying to help."

"I know," he said through gritted teeth. "You've been trying to help ever since I got back from the hospital."

"Then why won't you let me help? I care about you."

He threw his hands up. "If you care about me, then leave me the hell alone. I can do this stuff for myself."

I bit my tongue as I watched him wheel over to the ladder and put it upright. It took him a while, but he was so strong he did end up getting it by himself.

After he was done he turned to me. "I'm gonna paint now," he said. He picked up the can and a screwdriver to pry it open.

I pursed my lips, then decided to tell him what my plan had been. "If you want to do that, then fine, but I came down here to offer to take you to Clint's. I thought you might want to get out of the house or something."

Hunter stopped what he was doing and looked at me, clearly thinking about it.

"If we're going to go, we kind of have to go now," I added. "I told my aunt I'd help with dinner later."

He thought some more, then put the paint can down and left the screwdriver on top of that. "Alright, let's go."

We stood there in silence for a moment. Finally, I walked out of the room to get my jacket and keys, my lips pressed tightly together as I did my best to avoid another argument. Hunter followed closely. Soon, we were out the door.

Neither of us spoke much the whole ride. Hunter turned the radio on almost as soon as he got himself situated, and we listened to the music rather than continue the discussion we'd started in the house. For my part, I didn't even know what I could say.

Eventually I caught myself daydreaming about what Marco's response to my letter might be. I shook my head, angry that I was letting him creep in again, and soon we were in front of Clint's Gym.

When we got there, I helped Hunter out of the car and told him I'd be back in a couple hours. Then I drove back home, thinking about everything that had happened to us. We'd almost been there. Almost happy. Hunter was going to get an apartment in Eltingville and we had everything figured out. Now we were back to the drawing board.

After parking his car in front of my aunt's house, I walked inside and was greeted by Rampage. I went to pick him up, but he scurried away to Hunter's room. Sighing to myself, I followed him in. He had managed to hide by the time I walked into the room. My guess was he had hidden underneath the bed.

As I got down onto my knees to look, something caught my eye. Hunter's gym bag was at the foot of the bed with his clothes folded neatly inside. On top of the clothes was a little black pouch. His MS treatment. The burden he carried with him everywhere he went.

My breathing quickened. I stood up unsteadily and plopped onto his bed, arranging myself so I was face down in his pillows. They still smelled like him. Memories of all the different times we had spent together washed over me.

Would the memories we made going forward be as good? How many more would there be?

Tears sprang to my eyes. Of course they would as good. I just had to figure out how to help us navigate us past this rough patch. Hunter's MS was in a bad spot, but that didn't mean I had to start acting like he was going to die any minute.

The more I thought about it, the angrier I got with myself. Hunter was the one with MS. It was him that was stuck in a wheelchair. I had to be the one who was strong and made this relationship work. He was already doing everything he could. He had enough on his plate.

I shook my head in frustration, tears still streaming down my face. Why couldn't I just focus on him? Even in the car earlier that day, I had drifted off thinking about Marco right after we'd had a fight. I wasn't even sure the fight was over.

No matter how hard I tried, I couldn't keep myself from crying. Anger crept up inside me anew.

Here I was, sobbing into Hunter's pillows, leaving them wet and messy. Hunter was trying to deal with being in a wheelchair and I was a sobbing mess.

How could I help him? How was I going to help myself?

I grabbed a pillow and pulled it tight to my face so I could scream into it. Why was I falling to pieces when Hunter needed me most?

Why?

Why?

WHY?

I turned onto my back and stared at the ceiling numbly.

This was just another step. I had to figure out how to get past this mess. I had to be stronger for Hunter.

Chapter Twenty-three
FRONT DESK

Hunter

I rolled into Clint's Gym in a shitty mood. Adjusting to the wheelchair had been more of a pain in the ass than I expected. It had only been a few days but I already hated being in this fucking chair. I could barely do anything for myself, which made me feel more and more like a burden on the people around me.

I was fucking things up again. Lorrie just wanted a healthy relationship, but it was hard to see a way to do that now. We'd almost had it, but now with my MS it was ruined.

Lorrie had worked her ass off for that art competition and she could've fucking won. Because of me, she couldn't go. How many other sacrifices was she going to have to make?

I knew she wanted to stay with me, but every time I thought about it, the more I realized how much she was giving up. My MS was totally unpredictable. It was impossible to make plans for the future when we didn't know when the next attack would strike. I wracked my brain endlessly for a solution, but nothing had come yet and I wasn't hopeful anything was coming.

Shaking my head, I rolled past the front desk. There was no point thinking about it anymore for now.

The desk was unoccupied again. I wondered if there were any days it was actually manned full-time. It was clearly still in use based on the papers and stuff, so someone came in at some point. Just not either of the times I'd been around.

Maybe Clint had his coffee there in the morning. The more I thought about it, the more it made sense it was just him that used the desk in the early morning. It was hard to imagine anyone putting up with Clint long-term. Or him putting up with anyone, for that matter.

I passed the desk and went into the gym. Guys were hitting the bag on the right and wrestling on the left, just like last time. Two were fighting in the ring, but to my surprise Clint wasn't there. I swiveled my head around. He was nowhere in sight.

After wheeling myself closer, I stopped in front of the boxing ring and watched the two fighters spar. They were both Hispanic kids, fifteen or so by my guess. Both were pretty skinny. Compared to the wrestling I'd seen before, these kids looked to have pretty good technique. The defensive skill of one of them in particular was sharp.

As I watched him duck and weave around his opponent's punches, I wondered if I would ever get to do that again.

"I see you got some new wheels," a voice said from behind me.

It was Clint. I turned around as quickly as I could. "Yeah," I said with a shrug. I tried to think of some joke to make about it, but I had nothing.

His blue eyes bore no trace of any pity. By the look of it, my newfound condition surprised him about as much as his alarm in the morning. "You down long-term? I don't see a cast or anything."

I looked down at my legs as if to confirm there was no cast. "Yeah. I mean, hard to say."

I took a deep breath. Clint waited patiently, seemingly with no place to go at all.

Might as well tell him. Couldn't pretend there was nothing wrong with me at this point. "I have MS," I said steadily. "Multiple sclerosis."

I watched for his reaction but he simply waited for me to continue, the corners of his eyes wrinkled in polite attention.

"Normally I just have to manage it, but I had a flare-up," I continued. "This was the worst one I've had. Is the worst one, I guess. So I'm stuck like this, for a while at least. Hard to say how long it will last."

Clint nodded and thrust his hands into his jean pockets. "You doin' therapy or anything?"

I shook my head. "Not yet. Gotta go back to the doctor in a couple weeks. If my tests are good, they'll let me start doing therapy."

Clint shook his head. "Hell of a disease, son. Best of luck to you."

"Thanks," I replied. "I was wondering if you'd still let me come in and do some coaching."

Clint shrugged and looked me in the eye. "If you can. Can't promise I'll pay ya if you can't do it, but I'm happy to give you a shot."

I nodded. "I appreciate the chance."

"You're welcome. Where's that nice girl you had with you last time? I'm guessing you don't have your car set up to drive yourself yet."

"She dropped me off," I said, my smile disappearing from my face. "I'm actually staying with her family at the moment. Long story."

His eyebrows shot up. "You're lucky to have that kind of support. I'll tell ya, a partner in life is the greatest blessing in the world."

"Yeah."

I knew I should have more to say about Lorrie than that, but I couldn't muster anything else. I turned and watched the kids wrestling against the wall. Even though they weren't very good, they could all probably beat me right now with my useless legs. I wondered when I would get my strength back to be able to take them again. Maybe I never would.

Clint broke into my thoughts. "Son, I know that look, and I don't like it. I'm gonna give you some advice: cut out the bullshit."

Blood rushed hot to my face. I shook my head. Why was he talking like he knew me? "What look? I don't—"

"Shut up and just listen. Every second you spend wishing you weren't in that chair is one you could spend living the life you have, and that should start with taking care of your relationships with the people that love you."

"Who said I wasn't taking care of those relationships?" I asked, my pulse pounding.

"I did. Call it an old man's intuition. You gonna tell me I'm wrong?"

I opened my mouth then shut it, too stunned to come up with a rebuttal.

He seized on my silence. "Listen, son, I know you're in a rough spot right now and I'm trying to help you. Take care of things on the homefront before you go picking any new fights. Which in this case I'm guessing is whatever it takes to get yourself upright again."

"Thanks for the advice," I said, my tone clipped. I didn't need a lecture from Clint.

He paused and looked away for a second before turning his steely gaze back on me. "I buried my wife last year. Married her right before I went to 'Nam. She waited for me the whole time." He shook his head. "I can tell you for a fact that you're blessed to have someone in your life. Greatest fortune a person can have. Cherish every day of it."

My jaw tensed. "I'll do my best."

He looked down at his shoes for a moment before bringing his head up again, his lips tight. "We all spend half our life getting up, son. Once we're stood straight, we have a look around, enjoy the view, and if we're lucky we die peacefully. It's a lot easier to stand up with someone by your side, and the view's a lot better. You don't wanna get to my age and wish you had done better by the people you love. Trust me."

I felt like I should say something, but he'd worked up a head of steam. "Every day," he said, pounding his fist from emphasis. "If you have someone to come home to who loves you, life will be happy. If you don't, good luck figuring it out. It might be possible, but I'm sixty-eight years old and I don't have a god damn clue how to do it."

I started to respond, but something in his tone made me stop. His words rattled around in my head while I tried to figure out why it bothered me so much.

He bit his lip for a moment. "Give me a call when you're feeling up to coaching," he said, his voice shaking slightly. "I gotta go teach these kids how to avoid getting their asses kicked, but you can stay as long as you like."

With that, he turned and walked to the ring.

I sat there, shaken and confused as I watched him get in and start coaching. Why was I so affected by the old man's speech? I'd been pissed off when he was giving it and now I couldn't get it out of my head.

I was still thinking about what Clint had said when Lorrie texted about an hour later to tell me she was out front. Before I left the gym, I passed by the desk in the building's entrance. To the right of the computer monitor perched on the desk was a picture of Clint and a woman with long brown hair. They were at a party and smiling wide. She must've been his wife. Was she the one who used to sit here at the front desk?

I glanced at the photo again. The two of them looked so happy and in love. It was sad to think about the short time the people in that picture had left together.

Chapter Twenty-four
DISTRACTION

Lorrie

Eventually, I got out of his bed and cleaned myself up in the bathroom. Even though I did my best, my eyes still looked puffy. Soon it was time to pick Hunter up at the gym. After finishing up with changing his pillowcase, I left, still spinning my wheels on how I could get past my obsession with Marco. The best I could think of was to ask my therapist about it the next time I saw her. For now I was an empty, exhausted husk.

I arrived at the gym and sent Hunter a text to let him know I was outside. A few minutes later he came out the front entrance. We exchanged short greetings and then I helped him into the car in silence. Once we were situated, I backed the car out and headed for home.

"Hey, thanks for taking me," he said, once we were on our way.

I pursed my lips and nodded absently. At least he was in a better mood.

My mind wandered to the letter I'd sent Marco. Maybe I shouldn't have been as cold. Maybe I should have pretended to forgive him, and then coaxed it out of him once I'd built up some trust. Would I have been able to do that? Maybe I could send him another one. I wished I could track whether he'd received the one I sent.

We came to a red light. Hunter looked at me curiously, his face concerned.

"Were you crying?" he asked.

My jaw clenched. "What makes you think that?"

"Your eyes are puffy."

I glanced up at the rear view mirror. He was right. No point in lying about it now.

"Oh. Well, yeah I did cry a little bit. Just being emotional. I'm fine."

He looked skeptical, but said nothing. We continued driving. I was glad we weren't continuing our fight from before. At this point, I wasn't sure I could take it.

I drifted to thinking about writing another letter to Marco. Maybe I could call the prison to see if the first one had been received. If I ever had to write another one, I was definitely paying for tracking information.

". . . said some stuff and I got to thinking."

Hunter was talking to me.

"Hm?" I asked, trying to pay attention.

"I said, Clint and I got to talking."

"Oh, what did you talk about?"

My voice felt distant, even to myself. I did my best to push Marco from my mind and focus on Hunter. Why was I trying to put my emotional stability in the hands of a murderer? What good could possibly come from that?

On the other hand, I clearly couldn't move on without some sort of closure. I had to find out why Marco did it so that things would start making sense again. Would I ever find out or was I going to be trapped by this forever?

". . . really care about you. I don't want to look back on my life wishing I had treated you differently."

Hunter was staring at me. He shook his head in frustration and let out a heavy sigh. "Lorrie, are you even listening? I'm trying to apologize here."

I rubbed my eyes. "Sorry, yes. I'm listening. Thank you for apologizing. I care about you too."

He frowned. "What's going on with you? Why were you crying?"

We were already half-way home and I barely remembered leaving the parking lot. My mind felt like it was trapped inside a cloud. I needed to snap out of it, fast.

"It's nothing, Hunter. I'm sorry."

No matter how it happened, I had to get this obsession with Marco's motive for killing my mom out of my mind. It was popping up more and more and it had to stop if I was going to be able to give my relationship with Hunter the attention it needed.

"Why do you feel like you can't tell me?"

Hunter was worried about me, but I didn't want to talk about it. I doubted that talking about Marco would help get him out of my mind, but it would definitely give Hunter something more to worry about.

"I told you it's nothing."

He shook his head. "Lorrie, look, I fucking hate being in this chair and I know it's hard on you too. I'm just trying to take it one day at a time. Sometimes I'm gonna fuck things up, but can you be patient with me? I promise you, I'm gonna work my ass off to get outta this chair as soon as I can."

Hunter looked at me, his gray eyes focused and intense.

"It's okay, it isn't your fault."

"Like hell it isn't. I'm sorry I was being a dick earlier."

"No really, I just . . . nevermind. Let's talk about it later."

He studied me suspiciously for a moment, but he didn't say anything. When he realized that I had nothing else to add he sighed heavily and turned away to look out the window.

Somehow, I'd managed to make things worse. Hunter was doing everything he could to make this work while I kept messing things up. I scrambled for some way to save it, but everything I thought of sounded dumb. I had nothing.

I bit my lip and glanced over at him before returning my eyes to the road. Even though we were sitting only inches from each other, it felt like we couldn't be further apart.

Chapter Twenty-five
ANSWERS

It was awkward between me and Hunter for the next few days. Every night, I'd have nightmares, and every day I would walk around in a fog. Aunt Caroline and Uncle Stewart seemed to notice the shift in our moods but gave us our space. I felt trapped in my own head. Even when I tried to focus on helping Hunter, my mind continued to drift back to thinking about Marco and my letter. I was thinking about asking my therapist for an emergency appointment.

Thursday afternoon rolled around. The two of us sat together in the living room, but neither of us felt like talking much. Aunt Caroline had left earlier in the afternoon to run some errands. She'd be coming back later after she picked the kids up from school. Uncle Stewart was still at work.

Hunter sat on the living room couch, watching TV. I sat beside him, a sketchpad open on my lap. After an hour, it was still blank.

Staring at an empty page wasn't going to help me. I sucked in a deep breath and decided to check the mail, just like I had every day that week.

"I'm going to go see if the mailman came," I said, standing up.

Hunter opened his mouth as if to say something, then he seemed to think better of it and just nodded. I turned and left. This was how it had been with us lately. On pins and needles.

I walked out the front of the house to the curb, opening the mailbox. There was a large stack of envelopes inside and I pulled them all out.

Coupons. Coupons. More coupons. Clothing catalog. Something forwarded to me from Arrowhart.

When I tore the envelope open, there was another envelope inside.

Cook County Penal System.

I froze in place, shivers running down my spine. My eyes scanned and rescanned the words as my chest pounded, blood rushing to my ears.

Marco had written me back. Finally.

My mind raced. Was this it? Was today the day I got some answers. After all my suffering, had I just needed to ask?

I tore the letter open and started to read:

Dear Lorrie,

I am very happy that you have written back. I want to to talk to you very much. I hope that one day we can understand each other.

I know you have a lot of questions and I will answer them, but you must come visit on May 11th. I will only tell you, nobody else. I am truly sorry. It must be on May 11th.

I spend a lot of time thinking about what I did and I only wish to find forgiveness now. Please find it in your heart to visit. It will help both of us move on to the next step. My PN is #276-2596. I put you on my guest list so the guards let you in.

With much love,
Marco

My heart sank. The date he gave me was the next day. It must've taken the letter a while to get to me. I was so close to getting the answers I needed, but he had to throw in one more step.

Still, though. The prospect of seeing him again face to face was scary, but if that was what I needed to do to get closure . . .

Why had it come now, when things couldn't be worse for Hunter and me? Was this a sign? Was this the way out?

I walked back to the house on autopilot, clutching the letter in one hand and the rest of the mail in the other. When I came inside I tossed the mail on the counter and stood there, rereading Marco's letter.

"Lorrie," Hunter said. "Hey, Lorrie. Is something wrong?"

I shook the fog away and saw him sitting in his wheelchair next to me. His brows were furrowed in concern.

"Huh?"

His eyes darted to my hand. "You walked into the house like a zombie. Didn't even hear me when I called your name. What's going on?"

Marco's letter was still clutched tightly between my fingers, a little clammy with my sweat.

I took a deep breath and tried to come back down to reality. "I'm sorry. I'm okay."

"What's that?" Hunter asked, looking at the letter with suspicion.

Even though I had been hiding the fact that my nightmares about Marco had been getting worse, it didn't make sense to hide it anymore when the end of our problems was so close.

I held up the envelope. "Do you remember the letter I wrote to Marco? Well, he just wrote me back."

"What did he say?" he asked, his eyes widening.

I didn't feel like explaining everything, so I just handed the letter over. "Read it."

He frowned and scanned it over quickly. When he was done, he cleared his throat. "I don't think you should go."

My face felt flushed. His response wasn't what I was expecting. "Why?" I asked, louder than I meant to. "What if I want to go?"

"Something about it just doesn't feel right," he said, shaking his head. He had softened his tone, but I could tell he felt pretty strongly about this.

I didn't say anything. This was the lifeline I had been looking for and now Hunter didn't want me to go. A million things ran through my mind as I thought about how to explain to him how important this was for me.

Hunter sighed. "If he really wanted to give you some answers, why couldn't he write them in the letter? Also, why did he choose a specific date? I dunno. Something seems off."

I heard the words he was saying, but they didn't sink in. All I could think about was the nightmares stopping. I could finally have some answers. An answer. That was worth the risk to me.

"I have to know," I said. "It's been driving me crazy, especially lately. I've been having all these dreams at night, and I've been daydreaming about it during the day, and I can barely think about anything else. If there's any chance he will give me an answer, I have to try."

He grimaced. "I dunno Lorrie, I really don't wanna see you get hurt again by this guy. He kinda seems like a psycho."

"I have to try!" I yelled. "I just have to! If it works, I'll be free from this. I haven't been there for you recently as much as I'd like to be, and it's because I haven't moved on from what happened to me yet. Don't you see? Once I get the answers from Marco, I can finally just concentrate on us. On you. And why did the letter come now? Just when we need answers the most? It's a sign . . . "

I babbled on while Hunter reached his arm around my waist and hugged me tight to him. I started to push him away, but then stopped. It felt good to be in his arms.

"Lorrie, shh . . . sh . . . it's okay. It's okay. Just don't rush into it. It's tomorrow right? Just sleep on it and you can decide in the morning."

I'd gotten myself so worked up I was shaking. "Okay," I said, trying to stay calm, but my mind was already racing ahead. The end to all of our troubles was close. I could feel it.

Chapter Twenty-six
TOSS AND TURN

The rest of the day drifted by at a snail's pace. I didn't tell anyone other than Hunter about the letter. I hadn't even decided what to do yet and I just knew that if Aunt Caroline found out, she would freak out.

Even though I managed to pretend to be normal the entire day, my mind kept weaving its way back to the letter. Was he really going to tell me if I went? What would he do if I left him waiting?

Hunter kept trying to catch my eye at dinner, but I avoided him and focused on my food the whole time. My aunt and uncle were continuing to try and give me space, so my silence didn't get commented on. The general feeling in the house was a mixture of awkwardness and tension. Even the kittens seemed to be staying out of sight.

Dinner gave way to innocuous family time with the TV on and Billy and Joel horsing around, blissfully ignorant of any reason things should be any different than they were. Finally, everyone got ready for bed. I said goodnight thinking I would probably want to go to the prison the next day. Even if I was going to leave the final decision for when I woke up, that was how I was leaning.

I changed into pajamas, turned off the lights, and got under my covers.

And tossed.

And turned.

And failed to even begin to drift off. I lay on my back and stared at the ceiling, feeling my heart race.

Adrenaline surged through my veins like I was running for my life, but all I was doing was trying to lie still.

Visions of Hunter's expression as he tried to catch my eye at dinner ran through my mind. He looked worried. We'd been on pins and needles since we'd gotten back from the hospital, and it wasn't getting better.

It wasn't our fault. We were both trying hard, Hunter especially. Life was just awkward at the moment because we both had things outside of our relationship that were really weighing on us. Hunter's problems were way more immediate than mine and they weren't going anywhere. If I could just shed my obsession with Marco, I could focus more completely on Hunter.

I turned over onto my side and buried my face in my pillow. Tears emerged from my eyes and wet the pillowcase before they even had a chance to roll down my cheeks. Frustration welled up in my chest. I breathed in and out heavily, trying to calm down. What choice did I have? I had to take a chance on getting rid of this voice in my head asking *why. Why?*

Why?

When I rolled onto my back, I felt wide awake. Dawn was cracking through my window. Maybe I'd managed to sleep for a while, or maybe it was adrenaline, but I was full of energy.

I sat up in bed. Whatever sleep I'd gotten was all I was going to get. I shrugged my covers off, stood up, and flicked the lights on.

Before I knew it, I was getting ready to go. It was time to face this.

I thought about whether to tell Hunter I was leaving. He would probably want to come with me for support, but I wasn't sure I really wanted him with me.

Hunter would be as sweet and as supportive as anyone could ask, but for this I really just wanted some space. This was between me and Marco.

I settled on writing a note and leaving it on the kitchen counter. Unless there was some crazy delay, I would be back by lunch. It would be just like I'd slept in. Our problems would be over by that afternoon.

Once the note was written, I headed out.

Chapter Twenty-seven
WHAT'S MINE TO KNOW

The sky was overcast as I drove to the prison. There were a lot of people on the road, especially for a Friday. Sitting in the stop and go traffic gave me time to think. That was the last thing I needed.

I hadn't seen Marco since the trial, at least not in real life. My dreams had been haunted. Now that nightmare was going to be made into a reality, and I didn't know if I was ready. At this point, though I didn't have a choice. I needed to understand why my mom had died. If this could get me that, then I would put up with anything.

Traffic finally cleared as I got past an interchange and began the final trek toward the exit for the prison. I caught myself grinding my teeth and opened my mouth wide, trying to get some of the tension out. It was no use. As soon as I closed my mouth, there I was, grinding again. Eventually I stuck my tongue in between my front teeth to try and stop my jaw clenching. That helped.

I thought again about Hunter. He might be a little mad when he realized what had happened, but at the end of the day this was between me and Marco. A glance at the clock told me it was just a few minutes before seven-thirty. I would probably get back before ten-thirty. At worst he was going to miss me for an hour or two. That wasn't the end of the world, Hunter would get over it.

This was just something that I needed to do. When Hunter had come to rescue me after the mess we had left in Studsen, I thought that all we needed to build a future together was to face our problems. We had made a lot of a progress, but clearly there was still something I hadn't gotten over. Going to see Marco would fix that. I'd be able to move on, and then I could go back to helping Hunter face his MS. He needed me and I needed to get over this one last thing. He was counting on me, I couldn't let him down.

Finally, the exit came and I got off. The road to the prison was littered with signs to beware of hitchhikers. Before I'd even thought about it, I locked my doors. The land was flat and treeless with nothing but fields in every direction.

After checking in at the gate and weaving my way to the correct lot, I parked my car. This was it.

Trying to steady myself, I emptied my purse of everything except my two forms of ID—my license and my Arrowhart ID—and the note with Marco's ID number on it. I double-checked everything, then put my purse under the passenger front seat and stared out the windshield.

Visiting hours started at seven-thirty, meaning I could go in whenever I was ready. I watched a small family filter in and steadied myself to do the same.

I thought for the millionth time about what he was going to say. Why had he done it? What did my mom ever do to him? The questions had eaten away at my dad until he'd been driven crazy. I didn't want the same thing to happen to me.

I opened the car door and tried to get out before realizing I had left my seatbelt on. My chest feeling slightly bruised from the sudden jerk of the belt across my chest, I sat back, undid my seatbelt, and got out of my car.

The parking lot was poorly maintained. Weeds sprouted from cracks in the asphalt. I caught motion from the corner of my eye and nearly jumped. When I noticed what it was, I shook my head. It was just a cat. Its black fur shimmered in the early morning light. For a split second I had the bizarre thought that it was the same one I saw around Lake Teewee before I fell in.

Taking a deep breath, I shook the idle thoughts out of my head and walked across the parking lot to the visitor's entrance. I was actually doing this. My heart thumped against my light jacket as I worked to steady my nerves and opened the door.

Even though I had arrived only ten minutes after the beginning of visiting hours, there was already a line of a dozen people waiting to check in. I got in the back and waited, my shoulders tense.

The drab beige walls and brown linoleum floor weren't unexpected, but the decor was depressing all the same. All but one of the people in line were women. Several of them had brought small children.

Everyone there was very excited about their visit. The emotion in their voices as they shared the pain of having a loved one incarcerated made me feel awkward. Then one of them spoke to me.

"Is this your first time?" the woman asked. She had dark hair and wore a lot of makeup, but her eyes were kind. By my guess she was in her thirties.

I nodded, unable to say anything more.

"It's not so bad. They'll check you in and pat you down, then bring you into a separate room. You can even give your man a little kiss and a hug if you want. It ain't like the movies with glass separating you or nothin'."

My stomach felt queasy. I knew she was trying to help, but what she said only made me more uncomfortable. There was no glass? I was going to have to sit in the same room with Marco and not even have a pane of glass to separate us?

She cocked her head and looked concerned for a moment. "He's not in segregation or anything is he?"

My throat felt dry and shut tight. I shook my head and dug through my reserve of willpower to try and be polite. I attempted a response but the words just wouldn't come out. My knees shook, and I steadied myself against the wall. Something oily and slimy crawled in the pit of my stomach and I wanted to throw up. I thanked myself for not eating anything that morning.

She put her hand on my shoulder. "Oh gosh, you're shaking. I'm sorry if I made things worse. Good luck with your visit."

With a pat on my shoulder, she turned and went back to waiting in line.

Chills ran up my sternum and down my spine. I'd already been on a knife's edge, but this was nearly enough to tip me over.

The line moved faster than I expected and suddenly I was up next. I dug through my pockets as the woman at the visitors desk waved me over.

She was heavy-set with short dark brown hair and wore brown wireframe glasses. To her credit, when she spoke it was obvious she was making an attempt to be cheerful.

"First time?" she asked.

I nodded.

"Okay, I'm going to need you to fill out this form and give it back to me with two forms of ID. You can just cut in line when you're done. Pens are over there."

I thanked her and took the form over to a nearby table. When I got there, I wiped the sweat away from my forehead and tried to focus on filling out the paperwork. The form mostly consisted of questions about my identity, the identity of the person I was going to visit, and whether I'd ever committed a crime or been to jail. Since I was clean on that front, it took very little time to complete.

After double-checking Marco's prisoner number at the top against the note I'd brought with me, I went back to the visitor's desk and handed my ID over with the form.

The attendant took it with a smile and entered the information from the form into the computer. I watched her work, keeping one eye nervously on the women who had gone to the next stage where they were patted down by a female prison officer before they were allowed into the visiting area.

Every second was bringing me closer to seeing the man who had destroyed my life. I knew he had the answers I needed. I just had to get through this and I would start to understand things again. I'd be able to start over anew with Hunter. We would be happy again.

"Ms. Burnham?"

The woman at the visitor's desk was speaking to me. Shaking my head, I gave her my full attention.

She pursed her lips. The previous friendly demeanor looked somehow strained. "You're here to see Mr. Peralta, correct?"

I cleared my throat. "Yes."

She pursed her lips and turned away. "Okay. One moment please."

I shifted awkwardly as she got on the phone and began speaking into the receiver. What was all this about? Was Marco in segregation or something after all?

After a couple minutes, she nodded and hung up. She put two fingers in her mouth and whistled for another guard's attention. His head turned and he came over quickly. He was a heavily muscled, dark-haired man with beady eyes and a buzz cut.

"Daryl," she said, "can you take this young lady to CR One please?"

Daryl nodded, apparently not needing any more clarification about his orders. "Follow me," he said.

As I followed him, my scalp began to prickle down to the nape of my neck. Why were they taking me somewhere different than everyone else has gone?

Was Daryl going to pat me down? A female had patted all the other women down, which I would definitely prefer. I didn't want to be felt up by some strange guy.

We got to the room. Daryl turned the knob and opened the door, stepping back to hold it for me. I held my breath and stepped in. Once I was in the room, he flipped the lights on for me, closed the door, and walked away. I could hear my pulse throbbing dimly in my ears.

What is going on?

I stood there, not knowing what to do as I listened to his retreating footsteps. The room had concrete walls that had been painted a creamy off-white and contained a single table with two chairs on one side and one chair on the other. The table was woodgrain laminate, the chairs black plastic. I took a seat on the side with two chairs, figuring the other side had to be the one for the inmates.

It wasn't until I was seated that I realized how small the room was. The table was maybe eight feet in length and four feet wide. It took up the majority of the room.

There wasn't much more space than was needed to scoot back your chair and get around the table. Marco and I would be in close quarters. I thought about where the prison guard would stand while Marco and I were talking. The palms of my hands felt moist with sweat. I wiped them against my jeans.

Without any windows, I began to feel a little claustrophobic. There wasn't even anything on the walls. This room was just a concrete box. My heart pounded against my ribcage.

I looked down at the table legs. They were bolted into the ground. I nodded to myself and looked at the door, but I didn't hear anyone coming. I supposed it took a while to go and get the inmate.

There was nothing to do but wait.

And wait. As I scanned the walls I noticed a clock above the door that nearly touched the ceiling. Once I'd become aware of the ticking noise, I couldn't get it out of my head.

I took a deep breath and tried to settle myself down. The clock ticked. My breaths became more shallow. I caught myself clenching my jaw. My tongue went between my teeth. I bit down. My hands were shaking and I couldn't steady them. I tried to tell myself that it would be okay. This would all be over soon, I'd get my answers and be on my way.

Footsteps came down the hall. I closed my eyes and tried to slow down my breathing, but my throat felt like it was closing off. The world began to spin like a top.

The door opened. I jumped even though I'd been expecting it. A man in a cheap-looking charcoal suit came in and closed the door.

He had wavy, black hair that was going gray at the temples and brown eyes. I couldn't read his expression and a jolt of panic surged through me.

"Lorrie Burnham?" he asked. His voice was raspy, like he smoked cigarettes by the pack every day.

I nodded, and he sat down.

"Lorrie, I'm Michael Rizzo with the Prison Bureau. I understand you are the stepdaughter of Marco Peralta. Is that correct?"

A shiver ran up my spine when I heard Marco's full name coming from someone else. "Yes," I answered shakily.

He nodded and clasped his hands together in what seemed to me to be a nervous gesture. My chest tightened until I was afraid I would need to lie down.

"Your stepfather was found hanging in his cell earlier this morning."

The room spun around me and my stomach felt like it was in freefall. "Marco?"

"Marco Peralta, yes. I'm sorry for your loss."

His words came from far away.

"But how?" I asked, trembling.

His hand came up to his mouth for a moment as if covering his expression. "For what it's worth, when they found him, he had a smile on his face."

I stood up, my legs unsteady. The news finally hit me, a dull throbbing pain starting in my gut. Panic seared through my chest and tears stung my vision. There would be no answers. I wouldn't be able to confront Marco and find out the reason everything had happened. There was nothing.

My heart hammered in my chest and I couldn't breathe. Sweat beaded on my back and I felt droplets slide down my spine, sending shivers through me.

Michael shot up to his feet and made his way to the door. "You can stay here," he said quickly. "I understand this has come as quite a shock."

"No," I said, barely able to muster a whisper. "Please let me go."

The room was too small and I couldn't stand another moment trapped in here.

"You're sure?"

I came to the door and stared at it, barely aware of his presence in the room. At some point, the door opened and I was led back out to the visitors area. I shuffled along in a daze, hoping that I could make it out of the prison before I broke down.

He was gone. When he had taken his life in that cell, he had locked the explanation for why he killed my mother away forever.

I was buried under the rock he'd left, and I would never be free.

Chapter Twenty-eight
STORM

I walked out into the parking lot, a hollow pain throbbing in my chest.

Rain had begun to fall from the sky while I was inside and the day had somehow gotten even darker. Water quickly soaked through my clothes as I trudged to my car, but I barely felt it.

I was lost. Marco was gone. I was never going to know what had happened to my mom. He had trapped me in a world that made no sense. Just like he did to my dad. Hunter had been right. Marco had wanted to torture me one last time. In fact, he'd been willing to take his own life to do it. My heart felt like it was being sliced open bit by agonizing bit.

Tears welled warm at my eyes and mixed in with the rain pelting my face from the sky. The parking lot seemed to go on forever. My shoes sloshed through puddle after puddle. I was wading through quicksand, unable to make any progress. My hair stuck to my head like a threadbare blanket soaked through.

Why did I even come? I was stupid. So stupid. How could I really think something good was going to come from this?

I'd thought this would be the last piece to get away from my tragedy and focus on helping Hunter with his condition, but now I had only made things worse and felt more lost than ever. Hunter still couldn't walk and I was spiraling downward again. I felt beaten and exhausted. Our happy ending had been doomed from the start.

I used the back of my hand to brush my hair out of my face, but it fell back down after a few steps. Sighing, I trudged along, keeping my head down so I could see.

A black cat scurried from the sidewalk where I walked. What was it doing out in the rain? I watched numbly as it scampered for cover under a parked Ford Explorer, also in black.

With my next step, my foot caught a crack in the sidewalk.

I tumbled over, unable to catch myself before I came crashing down onto my hands and knees. The impact hurt worse than I expected it to. I stayed there in shock for several seconds before rolling into a seated position.

My hands were scraped up, and my knees were going to be bruised. I sat and let the rain fall on me, gathering up the strength to stand.

A voice came dimly over the smack of the rain on the pavement.

"Lorrie!"

Barely lifting my head up, I wiped the water from my face and squinted. A wheelchair-bound figure approached through the rain. *Hunter*.

I looked away, my lips trembling. Why had he come? I was ashamed for him to see me like this. Hunter had warned me not to do this and I ignored him. He was the person who was dealing with a real burden and yet here he was, coming to save me after I'd hurt myself like a child.

Hunter practically skidded to a stop, he had been wheeling himself so fast. He was soaked. His black t-shirt already clung tight to the skin of his torso, making his abs visible through the fabric as he breathed in and out.

"Lorrie," he gasped, breathing hard. "Are you okay? What happened?"

I sat there, mute, and a sob swelled up in my chest. Everything came crashing down on me as I tried to put into words what had happened. My body convulsed as the sob broke free.

"Do you want to go back to the car? Your uncle drove. He's waiting in the parking lot. Come on, we gotta get out of the rain."

Hunter was almost shouting so that I could hear him over the roaring of the rain, but his words barely registered.

I continued to cry. Every time I got my breath, I tried to tell him what had happened, but the words caught in my throat and were swallowed by another sob before I got the chance. Drops of rain splashed against my face as I tried to speak.

Hunter bent down and took my hand carefully in his, seemingly waiting for me to calm down. It took a few minutes. We were both soaked, but he didn't even seem to notice the rain. Finally I was able to choke something out.

"Killed himself," I said, before another sob took hold of me.

"Marco?"

I nodded.

He put his other hand over mine, his face grim. We stayed there for a few moments in silence. It felt like an eternity and yet like no time at all. The world around us passed by in a blur.

"I'm so sorry," he said.

I bit my lip, trying to steady myself and finally having a little success. "No, I'm sorry," I sobbed.

"What? What do you mean?"

The rain pounded down against my hair, matting it to my head. I wiped a thick strand away from my face and tried to tell him what I meant, but a fresh sob swelled in my throat and choked the words away.

"Lorrie, come on. Stand up. Let's get out of the rain and dry off. I'm here to support you."

Hunter pulled my arm up, trying to get me to stand but I couldn't get up. The world felt less than real. He finally managed to get me to lean on his legs, and I rested on them.

"It's never going to be over," I finally choked out.

He shook his head. "We'll get through it. Come on, let's get out of the rain."

But I couldn't move. The full weight of everything that Marco had done was falling in place and I was buried under.

"He did it on purpose," I murmured. "Why? He knew I'd come and he knew this would hurt me the worst way he could."

Hunter squeezed my hand tighter. "I don't know Lorrie. I wish I did."

"Now he's won. He killed my mom, that killed my dad, and now . . . " I trailed off. Tears streamed endlessly down my face and sobs shuddered through me. When I'd sucked in a few breaths, I tried again. "It's not like this was some accident. He had it out for my family. For me. Why?"

"I don't know, but we gotta move on. We can't stay here."

Didn't he understand? I'd already tried to move on and ignore it. That hadn't worked. Now I'd tried to confront it head-on, and that hadn't worked either. What was left? Nothing. I was stuck with being haunted and there was no way out.

The rain picked up, coming down in sheets against the pavement and on the cars nearby. It made a deafening amount of noise.

"Lorrie, are you hearing me? Stand up and let's go. We've got the rest of our lives to live."

I began to cry more, the tears forming salty rivers down my face. His words were making it to my ears but I couldn't absorb them. I buried my face in Hunter's lap. He treated me far better than I deserved, even when he was going through so much.

His jeans were soaked and only made my face more wet. I bawled into his legs, wishing everything would go away.

He let me cry and didn't say anything for a while. After I'd cried myself out, I wiped away my tears until there was only rain water left on my face. I was numb and empty. There was nothing left inside me.

Then his voice got low and took on an edge I'd never heard in it before. "I'm sorry you didn't get the answers you wanted today," he said. "Sometimes, things happen to us that we never understand and we worry we'll never get back to normal. But there is no normal, Lorrie. All we can do is move past the pain and hope that we have someone to stand next to us."

He stared into the distance, and then shook his head.

"I'm never gonna understand why I have this disease and I'm never gonna know what the future holds for me. For a long time I was scared of that. But I'm not scared anymore. You know why?"

I sniffled, but didn't say anything.

"Because of you."

I turned away, trembling. Why did he think it was because of me? I could barely keep myself together.

"Look at me Lorrie," he said, putting his hand on my cheek. His gray eyes glimmered. "Yes. It's because I love you. I love you so much that it hurts. We're going to be together for . . . for as long as we can. I won't say forever, because none of us have forever. But I want to be with you right now. And right now. And right now."

He brushed some of my hair that had fallen over my face behind my ear.

"The only thing I want is to live in every moment I have with you standing by my side. Wherever you go, I wanna be there with you."

I half-heartedly tried to pull myself up by grabbing the arms of his wheelchair, but slipped back down and fell hard on my butt. I shook my head. Marco had won. I would never know why my mom had been killed. I would keep being haunted. Nothing was going to change.

"I don't know—" I mumbled, shaking. "I don't know if I have anywhere to go from here."

His face locked into intense focus as he stared into my eyes, his own gray irises aflame. He leaned his forehead against mine, his breaths coming in short bursts.

"Yes you do," he said, his voice rising with every word. "Yes you do, because you have me, okay? YOU HAVE ME!"

With a growl, he leaned forward and put his hands under my armpits. He pulled me up toward him until I was on my knees and my head was on his chest. Then he brought his hands down to the armrests of his wheelchair. His legs flexed to stand up and I gasped, draping my hands reflexively around his back.

He grit his teeth, shaking with effort, and began to rise. His face locked into an intense grimace as he slowly straightened his legs.

Seeing him struggle shocked me into action. I couldn't let him lift both of us up. Even though my legs still felt weak and my knees hurt, I stood upright.

Together, we came to our feet, his head eventually rising above mine. I buried my face into his chest and his chin came to its familiar spot atop my head. For a moment, we held each other.

Then suddenly, his knees buckled. My arms shot out to steady him. I pulled him to me until we were leaning against each other.

He swayed slightly and I could tell by his breathing that he was struggling hard to stay up. When he shifted more of his weight onto me, I stiffened my legs in response and leaned more into him.

He was heavy, but together we were able to keep him upright.

We held each other. I sobbed into his wet jacket, my heart swelling with hope. Hunter was standing.

I frantically pulled his mouth to mine. Our lips crashed together, the heated wetness of our tongues burning away the cold around us. This close to him, I could still smell his scent. It reminded me of the sweatshirt I stole from him on the wet, cold morning that we had met so long ago. When we broke away, Hunter was still looking straight at me.

"You have me," he said between heavy breaths. "As long as you have me, you'll have somewhere to go."

Hunter had been right. We could save each other. We already had.

"And you have me," I said, showering his face with kisses. "I love you, Hunter. I love you. I love you. I love you." When I was done, I rested my cheek against his face, as his warm hand rubbed my back.

We leaned on each other as the rain storm roared around us.

Chapter Twenty-nine
CLOSURE

I stood on dirt road running through the middle of the cemetery with flowers in my hand. The sun was poking through the clouds after a brief summer rainstorm. The ground smelled like freshly turned earth. Birds had come out to begin singing again after the brief interruption. The world was full of life.

It took a while for me to find the spot, but in the end I remembered where it was. I stood before it solemnly and bowed my head.

"Hi guys," I said quietly. "It's been a while."

My eyes shot back and forth between the headstones of my parents. They had bought these plots next to each other before they divorced, and with the sudden nature of their deaths that never got changed. I thought it was fitting. Even though they couldn't be next to each other in life, at least they lay beside each other in death. I wished yet again they had never gotten divorced.

Shuddering, I took a deep breath. "I'm okay," I told them. "I want you guys to know that. Life has been really hard without you, but I'm okay."

A hand rested on my shoulder. I turned to Hunter, who was standing by my side, even if he needed crutches. It had been three months since his last MS attack, and he had exceeded all expectations in physical therapy. The doctors were confident he would be walking without crutches again. Maybe even in the next few weeks.

I turned to him and he smiled, giving my shoulder a tight squeeze. I smiled back at him before turning back to my parents' graves.

"For the longest time I was trying to recover. Trying to get back to normal. But that's never going to happen for me, really. What happened to you guys is just part of my life now. It took me a long time, but I realized I can still be happy."

Tears began to fall from my face, but I wasn't ashamed of them. Some things were worth crying about. I paused to dab at my eyes with my sleeve.

"I miss both of you guys so much. If you were alive, I know we could find happiness in our own way. Even after the divorce. We would have made it work. I know it."

I pressed my lips together and wiped my eyes again.

"But you're not here. So I'm finally finding another way to be happy, like I know you would have wanted. Even when you got divorced, I never doubted you both loved me and wanted me to have the best. And I found him."

I put my hand over the hand Hunter had on my shoulder and smiled at him.

"I know both of you would like him," I said.

When I thought of my father's expression if he were to ever meet Hunter, a laugh bubbled up in my chest. He had always been so hyper-focused and business-like. I knew he would come around on Hunter, but his first impression probably wouldn't have been the best. "Even you, Daddy."

I chanced a glance over at Hunter. He cleared his throat. "I'll take care of her," he said solemnly. He readjusted his crutches and put an arm around me.

Leaning into him, I turned back to the headstones. "I love you both. I hope wherever you are, you're at peace."

I put my head down for a moment of silence. Hunter followed suit, and we stood there together, paying our respects to my parents. So much had happened since my father took his life. Since I'd met Hunter. Since I'd left Arrowhart. My life had turned on its head more times than I could count, but I'd pulled through. It was mostly because I'd had Hunter by my side.

After a moment of silence, I kissed him on the cheek. "Thanks for coming here with me. Let's get back to the car."

We walked, or swung on crutches, or whatever, back to the car. Side by side.

Epilogue

Hunter's head popped up from under the water. He was just a small dot out on the blue waves of the Pacific Ocean. His long muscular arms started to beat against the water as he swam back towards the shore.

Hunter had started walking without his crutches over a year earlier. Even though he was done with PT, he still worked on his legs regularly at the gym, and they were already almost back to normal strength. We were both incredibly grateful that his disability had only been temporary. His legs had healed remarkably quickly, the doctors said that it was a combination of his overall health and positive outlook.

I leaned back my towel, the heat of the hot sand seeping through it, and let the sounds of the beach wash over me. Seagulls screeching in the distance. Children chasing each other around sand castles. The soft lapping of the waves against the shore.

When I looked back at the shore again, Hunter was already out of the water and walking up the beach in his red trunks.

His ripped body glistened with droplets of water, from his huge shoulders to his chiseled chest. It made his sexy tattoos stand out even more. Even though I couldn't help but notice other women staring at him, he only had eyes for me. He gave me a little wink and I grinned back.

I had my art history book closed next to me. When we were getting ready to come down to the beach, I had made plans to study, but I hadn't even cracked it open since we'd gotten here. It would be okay, I only had half a semester left before graduation anyway. I was closing out the end of my final semester at the UCLA Arts and Design Program. I had to take a lot of extra classes since I hadn't taken many art classes at Arrowhart, but some of my credits transferred so I didn't need to stay for the full four years.

A shadow blocked out the sun and I looked up to see Hunter's grinning face, his wet hair draped across his face.

"Hey Snorrie, don't tell me you're going to just keep sitting in the sand. You haven't swam at all today!"

"Yeah?" I asked, feeling playful. "Are you going to make it worth my while if we get in the water?"

Hunter raised an eyebrow and lowered himself over me, leaving a soft, tender kiss on my lips. I could smell his scent even underneath the salty water. "Maybe, you'll just have to come and find out," he breathed into my ear.

I giggled as his breath tickled the side of my face.

"Okay, let's go," I agreed. I got up, taking his hand as I rose. We walked slowly down the beach towards the water.

I smiled at the attention we were getting. Even though Hunter wasn't fighting anymore, he still stayed in very good shape. On top of that, he was a lot more tan. I guess I was too. Hunter was coaching at a popular MMA gym downtown. He had been able to use his experience working for Clint to get the job. Sometimes I went to see him, and he always had a smile for me when I came in.

The progression of Hunter' MS had been managed pretty well too. He was really taking good care of himself, watching his diet and stress levels, and being prompt with his treatment regimen.

Hunter slapped me playfully on the butt. I tiptoed up and gave him a kiss on the cheek.

"Aw, thanks. What was that for?"

I shrugged. "I don't know. Just because."

He kissed me on the cheek in return and I grinned so hard my face hurt.

Looking up at the sun beaming down on us, I hoped that Daniela was having as good of a time as I was. She had gone off to join the Peace Corps with Kyle. Now they were both serving their two years in Peru before Kyle went off to med school and she went to get her Ph.D. in Psychology.

I didn't talk to Aunt Caroline nearly as much as I used to, but I still checked in from time to time. Bones and Frida were fully grown now and getting into all sorts of mischief. My cousins had been really happy that they were able to keep two of the cats.

As for the rest of the litter, we gave Iceman to Gary—who had since apologized to me for some of things he'd said at Hunter's last fight. It was harder to be forgiving towards Ada, but even I realized that she did care about Hunter, in her own way. She did seem to be a lot friendlier to me after we gave Georgia to her. Maybe cute kittens were the solution to many of life's problems.

And then there was Taylor and Rampage. They were at home in the small one bedroom apartment I shared with Hunter. Hopefully they were only scratching at their new cat castle, and not the furniture. The four of us made our own weird little family.

Cool water lapped at my toes, and I realized that we had reached the shore.

"Tag, you're it," Hunter said, tapping me on the shoulder and sticking his tongue out at me. Then he ran into the water all the while doing his best impression of a maniacal evil genius laugh.

I laughed and chased after him. When the water was too deep to keep running, I started swimming after him, taking long slow strokes. The temperature of the water was just perfect and it felt refreshing against my skin.

When Hunter finally slowed down, I was able to reach him. We both tread water about fifty feet away from the shore. I stared into his gray eyes and gave him my best bedroom stare. He gave me a goofy grin, and I brought my face closer to his. Leaning in, I left him a sensual wet kiss on the lips.

"Now you're it," I whispered into his ear.

Then I ducked my head under and dove deeper into the water, letting air slowly out my nose. When I couldn't hold my breath any longer, I took a few strokes back up towards the light and broke through the surface.

Thank you for reading!

If you could spare a moment to leave a review it would be much appreciated.

Reviews help new readers find my books and decide if it's right for them. It also provides valuable feedback for my writing!

☺

Sign up for my mailing list to get discounts, exclusive teasers, and to find out when my next book is released!

Find me on Facebook:
https://www.facebook.com/priscillawestauthor

Made in the USA
Lexington, KY
09 November 2014